STAND IN HELL

Dennis E. Bolen

Random House of Canada

Canadian Cataloguing in Publication Data

Bolen, Dennis Edward, 1953-
Stand in hell
ISBN: 0-394-22402-7
I. Title.
PS8553.O54S73 1995 C813'.54 C95-930218-2
PR9199.3.B65S73 1995

Printed and bound in the United States.
10 9 8 7 6 5 4 3 2 1

In memory of
Elwin

Drink in Heaven,
Stand in Hell.

In 1938, Dad, you kept it away from us, but in 1938 Grandad left for the old country after the death of his wife and other setbacks, not the least of which were crop failures and the bad years of the Depression. You were twelve. You were taken out of school. You had to work. Grandad didn't get back 'til 1947. He was only supposed to be gone for the winter, but he didn't come back for almost nine years. He said he got caught in the war, but looking back on it, that couldn't have been the whole story, could it...?

1

For some reason you want to kill this dog.

I don't know, Grandad. I don't know the centre of it. I mean, I've been drunk.

Sure.

I've been angry.

Anyone who drinks like you and I knows the kind of anger I'm talking about.

But in all the research and all the stories in my head and all the goddamn driving, I'm no closer to it. The tale echoes for me — the way you tell it, the way Dad tells it, the books, the documentation, the evidence, the way I tell it to myself — but I can't get a focus. It wasn't until I heard this one about the dog, though, that I had any idea what to do about it. So here I am.

And I don't know if you care. I don't know what you think. I don't care, Grandad. You're a fucking asshole. Let's start from there and see if you come out any further ahead.

I speak with authority on this subject, if I do say so myself. I've been to see the land. I've seen the barn, the dust on the floor, the bullet holes still there after all these decades. I've been to the cemetery, and of course I've known a number of the major characters all my life. So see how it sounds to you, all this remembrance and research and observation and extrapolation.

Dad tells me that you and he — you still call him 'the boy', don't you? — you worked together in a lot of silence around the time of the illness of Lena Josephine. Prairie winter. The cold cruel on your feet, rattling your shins as you walked on the hard ground. The farm. Late in the thirties, despair-decade, etcetera. There was silence at work, keeping the machinery going, feeding the animals. There was silence at night, thinking before sleep. No sound but the faint swill of the bottle.

Could the boy hear it? Behind the thin curtains that passed for doors, he probably could. But that was a silence too, most likely. No need for talk there. You spoke a clear language and in my mind and memory it reels out like this:

There was the day in late winter when your wife was sick and Maisie the dog didn't do the work she was supposed to do, herding the cows. She frolicked near the gate and didn't respond when you yelled. The boy bounded along with a stick, coaxed the cows, ran into the yard and wondered where Maisie was. A shot that must have made him colder than the air rang from the barn. Two more shots — slaps on the ear, and you calling out.

"Still, you cur! Still…!"

More shots.

The boy looked in at the barn door, not wanting to

see: the whiskey smell on the air, you breathing hard, struggling to reload. Your eyes — red sores — looked up, then
down again to the weapon.

"Make that cur still!"

Maisie stared up at the boy, happy enough still, but
puzzled by the new game. She panted gently, twitching her
head, watching you sweat and fume with the rifle.

The boy did not speak. The dog puffed and there were
clicking sounds from the rifle. You levelled and fired again.
Maisie jumped, unhurt, and pranced to another corner of
the barn, a little alarmed but willing to play along.

The boy wanted to say "Papa..!"

You looked at him standing in the doorway, the light
behind hurting your eyes. You could see the fearful wondering in the boy's silhouette, the way his chin arched
toward his chest, the eyebrows. Staring, you lurched and
steadied yourself against a stall.

"Hold her!" you ordered.

The boy stepped ahead but then stopped, realising.

"Get in here." you gestured.

"Pa..."

"Get in here."

The boy went slowly to the dog, crouching, his hands
out to cradle her face. Maisie accepted the loving — more
familiar, better than the strange game with you. She sat and
took a rubbing about the ears.

The click of the gun froze the boy. He forced himself
to move around and see.

"Hold her...!"

You pointed the gun at the ground in front of the boy
and the dog, slightly to one side. You wavered, drunk. Your
eyes cast down for a moment, then rise, angry. "Back!"

The boy hardly had time to let go of the dog and step away. The shot crashed close to Maisie and she leapt, yelping, and clawed for another corner of the barn. You snapped off another shot as she went.

For a moment everything was still. You cocked the gun. The boy stood horror-frozen, staring. Maisie quivered in the farthest corner of the barn, nestled in some hay. She stared with darkened eyes.

You turned a bloodshot eye to the boy. With the pounding in your head you were becoming drunker and drunker as the seconds passed. You pointed to the dog, gestured with your head, and almost fell over.

The boy stepped toward you. Stopped. There is no father in your face. Your eyes closed in a bleary sigh. There were tears now, running down your face. From where we don't know. Times are tough. Nothing is going right. Soon there will be no wife. This land isn't like the old country. There are no relatives. There is no forgiving.

You need the boy around here. There's work to be done. Too much work. Too many problems. But you want to kill this dog.

You opened your eyes, wiped the moisture off your face with your gun-hand sleeve. For an instant the barrel points directly at the boy.

A tuft of dust rose at the door of the barn, dried muck kicked up by Maisie in her flight. The boy could see this was to be and he knew he would be there when it happened because he has endured the silence with you for so much of his life. The only thing is to do as we are told. Turn off, shut off, blank out, do what's necessary, but do as you are told. He strode to Maisie and crouched, stroking her.

As you approached, the dog tensed, ready to flee. The

boy gripped her haunches firmly, squeezing his eyes shut. He could sense you close, very close beside him. There was quiet: a father and his son and their dog in a barn. Then the trigger changed everything. The bullet entered Maisie's neck and the jolt ran up the boy's arms to his chest and into his heart, impairing that organ forever. Despite the future love of a good woman and sons, grandchildren, good friends and warm hearth-fires for fifty years and more, a relatively good life and other dogs, god knows, plenty of other dogs and children — frozen for good as the shocks flowed back down his arms, cramping his fingers into claws as you pumped a second slug into Maisie.

Now it came, the tears, sobbing. The boy held the twitching, struggling dog with all his might, but he couldn't tell if Maisie was whining or making any noise because of his own crying. There was a lot of sound now to mix with the silence as the boy let go and Maisie struggled to her feet and stumbled toward the door. You swore and kicked at her with a bloodied boot, aimed again and pulled the trigger, but it just clicked.

"Achh…!"

The dog collapsed on the dirty floor in the middle of the barn. You cursed and stomped outside, swinging the gun over your head, raging.

Now it was just the boy in the barn and the crying sound had gone with you. The boy gripped himself, thinking he might dirty his pants if he let go. He listened to the whimpering of Maisie and felt that he might let go anyway if he heard one second more. He ran to the dog, wishing her death, wishing to help, but how? The dog did not seem to see him, though her eyes were wide. She struggled to rise, hind legs whisking the frigid floor-grit. The dust rose higher and higher in the barn light. The boy saw your ballpeen hammer hanging at the tool bench and knew, even at this age, that what was about to happen would hurt him for a long time.

The wooden handle in his mitten-less hand was like another bone of his arm. As he walked to Maisie he swung the tool gently at his side and tried to see how he would do this. He knelt beside the dog and firmed his free hand on her wounded shoulder. The blood was hot near the wounds, cooling off fast where it had flown onto her coat. He could feel the life coming out of the holes, but not fast enough.

The first blow, meant for all his wishing to be the only one necessary, glanced off the dog's skull, shearing an ear, and slammed useless onto the floor. Maisie howled, terrorising the boy to panic. He bashed, desperate, pummelling with both hands. Not looking. Hoping.

Finally he returned to himself, sensing that it was now only he who struggled. He stopped, the hammer raised, and opened his eyes. Maisie was still, her head a mash of blood and hair. An eye was out and lay beside her open mouth. Steam rose. The boy looked but knew he couldn't. He closed his eyes but knew he would have to see, opened them again and looked away, up to the loft. He sensed a shadow in the barn and saw you beside him. You gently lifted the hammer from his hands. You, gunless, cried silently, the tears made muddy rows on your face. You crouched and embraced the boy.

"Sorry. Boy. Sorry. Sorry…" You cried audibly now. Your whiskey breath was so sour the boy gagged and thought he might vomit. "Boy, boy, boy…" Then silence.

The cold was now what spoke. A shiver clutched the

boy and he knew this business must end soon or he might not survive it. Stiffly, he rose to his feet with your arm still around him. You stood, unsteady, vacantly looking at the boy, then wandered from the barn, mumbling. The bloody hammer swung at your side.

The boy watched you go, then looked down to the mess. Straddling the dog, leaning down, the boy knew he must look this last time at his friend until the task was done. Then, he promised himself, there would be time to forget, to survive. The boy hefted the loose, warm body and staggered out of the barn, trying to grip only in the non-bloody places.

Walking slowly across the yard toward the woodpile, the boy decided to place the dog at a spot under a tree by the road to the slough. It was a place where, in summer, he came to read his books and eat a stolen apple. To dig in this place he would need the pick and shovel back in the barn. The ground was frozen so hard the pick would bounce off and send jolts up his arms. Fine. The least he could do. Maisie was a good dog. Still was a good dog. Her close warmth seeped into him and made the wind less cruel. The boy fought a tear, and struggled to hold up the dog. On the far side of the woodpile he gently laid her down, her head making an audible knock against the split logs.

The boy wanted to speak, if just for the tribute of it. Or maybe just to hear a sound other than those he had been hearing. He stood, looking at the dog.

"Poor Maisie, soon you will be like the wood."

In the barn he found the pick and shovel, but as he reached for them a shadow was at the door.

"Boy," you said, pointing to the yard. "Cows."

The boy stood, looked at the tools in his hands, and then looked back at you. On your face there was no sign of

the tears. The moment was over. Maisie the dog was past
and the silence now returned. The boy shivered. You moved
away from the door. The day was getting old; dusk
approached and the greyness of the sky promised snow.
The pick and shovel were returned to their places. The
cows would be milked.

A dead dog's body will stiffen quickly in such cold
until it is as hard as wood.

Morning chores began at six. Six is darkness on the Canadian
prairies at this time of year. It was even darker at five. The
boy emerged at this early time and darted to the barn,
fumbled a lantern alight and once again sought the tools.

At the woodpile the laden boy fidgeted again with the
light, turning it up, sheltering the flame from the gusty
wind. He firmed himself, preparing to find Maisie, bury her
and continue in the quiet, hoping for a better time somewhere past the dim sunrise that was coming in a few hours.

The lantern illuminated the wood, grainy and rough,
split and lying about. There was powdery snow blown into
the cracks between the pieces like some ghostly mortar. But
there was no dog. Maisie was gone. The boy searched,
turned the light up more, struggled amongst the wood.
Maisie was gone. He kicked at the wood, cursing. He
looked for tracks, bloodstains, loose hair, anything.
Nothing. He cried out, into the black sky. The cold ate
through to his heart and the wind sobbed at his ears and
made him alone, as alone could ever be.

2

Robin Wallenco remembers driving the highway into his hometown with pointless anger, gripping the wheel. He daydreamed sideways, arriving at the idea that it would be good to find a woman and fuck her savage and strange, but then tried to keep his mind on the present.

Robin's home town stank of the pulp and paper money machine and today it was sweltering hot, the heat backing against the mountains, letting no one escape. His teen years had gone by here. Permanent smoke rose from stacks. The kids worked in the mills and drove sports cars before they were bright enough to know they were terminal. The parents truck-and-campered their way to oblivion. Everybody doomed in the sulphuric vapours of straight-ahead industry.

Robin had never been part of the place. The first possible minute, he'd loaded up the beater and headed out of town.

He knew that Mom, and especially Dad, were puzzled and disturbed, expecting something bad, something tragic and emotional from him on this visit. Driving and thinking, re-clenching his hands on the wheel, a roiling started in Robin's stomach and moved to his gut, cramping.

At his parents' home Dad tensed back in his chair when Robin started talking.

"I'm not staying, Dad. I just want to tell you. You and I, we haven't talked…I want to say some things straight, here. Bad things are coming." But the more he tried to speak, the worse the pain in his intestines became.

After a while, Robin walked furtively away from the house, got into his car and left.

Home was a two-hour drive down-Island. The crisis in his bowels pressed against the time he would be in his own home and could take an urgent shit in the privacy of his own bathroom. He wanted to make it. He tried to think what would be available up ahead just in case he couldn't. For a few moments, heading out of town, he didn't feel so bad. He knew that he'd be better, shit or no shit, once he climbed that last hill, traced that last curve and was at last out of town.

Then it started again, weirdly gurgling intestines, abdominal convolutions against the waistband of his trousers. He struggled along, cramped into a crazy posture, trying to sit in a maximum cheek-squeezing position. This was little help. He was weaving the car back and forth over the road in a slalom of giddy torture. A clamminess covered his face, seeped under his shirt. He tried to think what to do.

Over the rise, on the extreme edge of town, was a motel they'd built since he'd moved away, a place with the obligatory 'Koffee Kitchen' family eatery and the kind of meeting rooms you could add or subtract by pulling movable walls around. Not the kind of place Robin wanted to stop.

A newer, nastier gut-stab melted any last resolve he had.

The lobby was air-conditioned pseudo-cold. Robin, shivering, not breaking stride, eyes searching for the washroom sign, noted that in the 'Cedar Room' at that moment the local chapter of the international *BRIGHTWAY* sales club was convening .

He spied the men's room sign and loped in that direction.

"Robin! Hey, is that you?"

Yes it's me, he thought, and you are you.

You.

Probably someone who stayed after graduation and got married and wears a baseball cap and to whom I wish every bit of luck but I'm sorry I can't talk now because I've got to take a massive shit and get out of this town.

Robin turned. It was a familiar face but its name was lost in the archives.

"Jeez, Robin. Been years."

The fellow's face was a smile-button, benevolent, genuine.

"Ten or twelve, I guess."

"Home to see the folks?"

"Right."

"Get back much?"

"Not much. Some."

"Still living down-Island?"

"Yup."

"Doin' the same work."

"Right."

"Well…"

Silence.

The schoolmate flushed, awkward at having run out of things to say.

The earnest will of his face made Robin regret. He tried to remember something he might have shared with this pleasing soul: a fun skirmish of murderball during P.E. class; a shared bit of daring during one of Robin's forays into illicit behaviour; drinking at a hockey game; drag racing fathers' cars out at the lake. But there was nothing aside from a general knowing that this fellow had been there during Robin's growing up. Now they were sort of all grown and they might have more to offer each other as friends of a common source. Comparers of notes. If only circumstances allowed. Then he thought of his father, and how they should do the same, and how impossible it would be, and how it would probably never happen.

Robin brought a sleeve to his forehead and wiped away the perspiration there, making sure no tears were leaking from his eyes. He shifted, one foot to the other.

"Still in town, huh? Doing okay?"

"Sure. Wouldn't leave it."

"That's good," Robin said.

"Hell, we got lots of work. Lots of places to go. Mountains and lakes. Got a nice wife and kids. Even pick up a little extra money selling *BRIGHTWAY*. Interested?"

"Huh?"

"Buying some stuff. It's a great product."

"Oh. No."

"Say, maybe you should sell this stuff yourself. You went to university didn't you?"

"Well yeah…"

"You'd be great at it."

"I don't think so…"

"I'll sign you up."

"Naw."

"Why not? Nothing wrong with making money."

"Look, I'm not staying. I gotta go." There was pain now. Robin doubled slightly forward, held his stomach and struggled against the cramps.

"Even better." The man's voice became commercially paternal, smooth as if squeezed from a tube. "We like to encourage out-of-town accounts. Where exactly is it you're living now…?"

"Look, I mean it." Robin took gentle hold of the man's sleeve. "I really gotta go."

"Nonsense." The man took Robin's arm and tried walking him toward the seminar room. "Don't worry. Everyone is shy at first. But you get over it quick. Just wait'll you learn the patented *BRIGHTWAY WAY* to success. The confidence! It spills over into your whole life." He winked. "Believe me."

"Whoa…" The pain was crippling. Robin turned, wrenching away from the man's grip. "Look, I can't remember your name — "

"Kenneth…"

"…Kenneth, but if you don't let me go I'm gonna shit my pants. Right here and now. Before the seminar."

Robin headed toward the men's room. Behind him he knew Kenneth would be watching him go.

"You can't run away from something like this." Kenneth's voice was still cheerful, selling.

Robin got to a toilet. He gripped the broken lock handle

of the stall, pulling to keep the door tight, trying not to be audible to others in the room. After a while, in pain but unable to release, the laughter started. He guffawed and then howled. He stopped, and the echo of his noises from the tiled walls reminded him of bombs.

He wondered what he would say.

3

Sebastian Wallenco pulled his near-new Lexus off the Island Highway and drove along the country lane. Approaching his brother's house, he noted with resignation the inevitable decay: unkempt grounds, ragged trees, car bodies strewn everywhere. Eviction, he could see it, sure as shit. Eviction for sure. Nothing like being the brother of a looney-tune — a vagabond wastrel renegade with nothing to run up against — to make a man dread what should be a fine time of drinking and dissipation.

Inside the house, things were not so bad. Mainly, Sebastian knew, because the place had not been lived in for a while. The rushing-water sound through the bathroom door told him Robin was taking a shower.

"Hey Robin," he yelled through the door. "I'm here."

No answer, the water rush continued.

Sebastian looked around. In the living room there was more than the usual clutter of papers lying around.

Flipping through, Sebastian saw that most of it was the family archives. He sat on the couch with a faded album and browsed through the sepia images. When Robin finished cleaning himself up he brought Sebastian a beer.

They sat together on the couch for a while, making the sounds of two men talking, laughing. Robin poured mineral water from a large bottle into a wine glass.

Sebastian drank his beer and looked around. "So, you drove down again?"

"It's the best thing I like to do. The best. Nothing like it…"

"Man, I'd like that too."

"Nothing like it. That open road. Those interstates. Best roads in the world. Terrific."

"How far'd you go?"

"Oh…Northern California. You don't know what it's like, driving like that. I mean…"

"Sure I know. I drive."

"Not like this. Not like I do when I'm on a roll. You just go and go until that feeling is gone. I mean it's great, man. Better than the babes."

"Oh yeah, the babes."

"Yeah, the babes. That's what I was talking about, not driving down to California, wasn't it?"

"Um…yeah. Either one, I don't care."

"But I gotta tell you about this one thing, what I started to talk about…"

"About the babes…"

"Well yeah, sort of but it's not really…Haven't you ever driven like that?"

"Like what?"

"Like, when you come to see me and then go home, you take the highway, you turn off at...Where?"

"Cowichan."

"...Cowichan. You slow down, signal the turn, ease off to the right and you're in the neighbourhood again, driving slow. You have to stop at the red lights. People walk by."

"Yeah. So?"

"You creep along the streets until you get to your condo and you stop."

Silence. Robin looked at Sebastian as if expecting him to brighten with the revelation.

Sebastian stared blankly. "The point, Robin. The point."

"Well don't you ever sense that pull to just stay on the highway and keep going?"

"Where to?"

"Wrong question. It doesn't matter where to. Who cares. The point is sometimes you gotta go. You gotta keep on the highway and let the car take its route, wherever it or you want to go, just to see where you end up."

"Is that what you do?"

"Sometimes."

"Well, I'm not like you."

Robin picked up his book of road maps from the coffee table and shook it at his brother.

"Don't you carry one of these around? Just in case?"

"No. What's that?"

"The official Rand McNally Road Atlas."

"Well, not for buzzing around town, no."

Robin flipped through the pages, admiring. "You never know."

"I know, most of the time. Maybe you don't, but I do."

"Naw."

"Well, like I said, you maybe."

"You bet."

"Look, this is weird. Since when did you start on all this free-as-the-wind stuff? I mean, you can't just go driving all over the place whenever you feel like it. What about school?"

"What about it?"

"I hear they're giving you an award. Best History Teacher, or something like that."

"So?"

"Don't you think that's exciting?"

"As opposed to what?"

"As opposed...? What do you mean, as opposed? It's great, that's what it is. I mean, when you were a kid nobody thought you'd ever do anything. Mom and Dad will be proud. I mean, it's better than what else has been happening..."

"What do you mean?"

"Well...You know."

Robin looked further at the road atlas, ignoring Sebastian, enraptured with the route-maps. "All those roads..."

Sebastian drank from his beer. "You were gonna tell me about this last trip. The girls..."

"Oh yeah, I got off track there...Anyway, shut up will ya, because I'm tired and I don't know how long I can remember this...Ummm..."

"The girls, the girls..."

"Yeah, I know, I'll tell ya, I'll tell ya, but I got this flash...It was something I wanted you to know about...What the fuck am I talking about? Oh, yeah. I'll always remember this. It's incredible. I can't believe it, it just blew me away, y'know, but it's there, right at this rest stop on I-5 just north of Salem there's this graffiti…"

"The writing on the wall…"

"Right, boy…" Robin jabbed a finger at Sebastian. "You read this writing on the wall, you see what it says to ya…"

Robin gravely gulped his water.

"Well? What did it say?"

"What did it say. That's good. What did it say… Man, that's just not deep enough. Not for this kind of shit."

"What did it say?"

"What did it say? You tell me. I'll tell you what it read." Robin paused, "It read *Jews Fuck Dogs*."

Sebastian put down his beer bottle, rose and walked across the living room. He stopped at the window, looking out, and said quietly, "I hope you're not going to start. I hope you're not going to start all this again."

"What does it say to you?"

"Never mind…"

"No, really, what does it say? It's different this time, I don't mean in a sociological sense or anything like that, although maybe I do, come to think of it. But take it one step further. Think about it. Who wrote it? Why?"

"It's disgusting! That's all there is to it. What's the big deal? Why are we talking about it? Again." Sebastian strode back to his chair, shaking his head.

"No. No. Seb…it's important to us, believe me. But look, I'm not trying to be heavy here. I'm sorry, but I was just…I started out talking about the babes and that brought this to mind. I know it sounds crazy. Bear with me. Huh? You can do that."

"Man-o-man. I don't know."

"Lookit, it's got a weird angle to it, believe me or not…"

"It's wrong. I don't want to hear about it."

"I know it's wrong! What do you think, you have to tell me it's wrong? I know it's wrong. That's the easy part Everybody knows it's wrong. But I'm trying to get you to see a kind of depth to the thing. There's a fabulous kind of literate structure to it…"

Sebastian noted the rising anger in Robin's voice. Grateful for a pause, he casually sipped his beer and shifted position in his chair. Robin stared at him with an expectant look on his face. Sebastian played with his beer bottle, scratching at the label with a fingernail. "Well, okay. If it'll see an end to this business."

"Good boy. You won't regret it. Anyway, I started out talking about the babes and this is relevant, believe me. But it strikes me that maybe I'm gonna have trouble getting it across to you. So wait a minute, this is great. Here's an example. I mean, have you ever known, like…a Jewish girl?"

"Quit it, Robin."

"No, this is important. You know what I mean."

"Yeah, I know what you mean. No."

"No?"

"That's the answer. No."

"Thought so. But that doesn't matter. Take it from me, I been with a couple of 'em. They're the best. Man! They're absolute tops. I mean, there's nothing like it. You get your hands on one of these sweeties someday, pal, you never let her go. Won't know what hit you. I don't know what they're like later on, you hear all the jokes, but man, the initial stages…Wild."

"Yeah, yeah, yeah. So what about it?"

"What about it?"

"Yeah. What about it?"

"Well it's pretty plain, isn't it? Use your head, it's pretty obvious. Look at who wrote that shit…"

"Who wrote it?"

"Yeah. Who. What type of person. You know."

"Assholes!"

"Exactly!"

"So?"

"So, the turd-head set thinks it spreads an inflammatory lie by proposing an obscene but unavoidable and probably subliminal image on the motoring public whizzing by. On the surface, anybody with half a brain can tell the content is more indicative of those who wrote than it is of those written about. But that isn't what I'm talking about! I'm talking about on a personal level, for a guy with my kind of background. The sign is not only a falsehood, but folds back in on itself like a collapsing Ping-Pong table. I mean, I know this is not true…"

"Yeah okay. Big deal."

"It is a big deal, Sebastian, little brother. Pal. It is a big deal."

Robin rose from his seat, grabbed the water bottle and stepped onto the coffee table holding his hands out, balancing.

"Oh, all right." Sebastian tried to appear not to notice Robin's action. "We've gone this far. Why is it a big deal? Tell me."

Robin closed his eyes and slowly brought the bottle to his nose in a mime of sobriety testing. He shakily succeeded. "It's a big deal, sport, because it's the first time I can remember that I didn't have to go on instinct, I didn't have to go on what people told me or what I had learned a long time ago. I just knew I was right, and that was it. I had the experience, the opportunity, the right and the will to make up my own mind." He opened his eyes, lowered his arms and looked down at Sebastian. Then he turned, readied himself and jumped in one leap from the coffee table over the couch, landing on the floor beyond without spilling a drop of water. He jumped to an about-face, and looked at Sebastian.

Robin said: "Whaddya think of that?"

Sebastian, snoring on the chair, started awake. He was in general pain, and realised he was shivering ferociously, wilting from exposure. He wondered if Robin's electricity had been cut off. Looking around, he noted the empty water bottle and many beer empties strewn around. Then the presence of another bottle, beyond the couch. Whiskey.

Robin slept face down on the couch, shuddering with cold but breathing deep. Sebastian creakily arose from the chair, went to him and nudged his shoulder. "Robin…"

Robin slept soundly.

"Wake up. Time to go to bed."

Robin did not stir. Sebastian shook him. "C'mon! Get to bed."

Robin did not respond. Sebastian shook him violently, turned him over, gripped his shoulders and shook, wrenching his brother's neck. Robin's rotten-plum stink of barley-mash assaulted him. He yelled: "Wake up! I'm not gonna carry you."

Sebastian drew back his hand and slapped his bother's face. No response. He slapped harder. Then again. Robin struggled and burped more booze breath. Feeling the booze, Sebastian forgot why he wanted Robin awake but could not resist the impulse to fire a solid blast with a closed fist at Robin's mouth. Then a flurry, and the men were clasped in staggering awkward restraints of hand and biceps, gasping hard and crying out. Sebastian, remembered himself, released his grip. Robin slumped back down to the couch, rubbing his eyes, waking, and stared at Sebastian.

Sebastian moaned and covered his face in his hands, rose and staggered away.

In contrast to Robin's squalor, Sebastian's apartment was always a neatness exhibit. He sat on his new forest green leather sit-wear, and spoke carefully on the telephone.

"I don't know... I don't know. No. I don't know."

The woman on the other end asked: "There's no way of finding out? What's the matter with you? You're his brother."

"Well you're his ex–wife. He listens to you."

"What's going on with you guys?"

"I don't know."

"Why should I get involved? Is he crazy?"

"No. Not yet. Aw, I don't know that either."

"Is he drinking?"

"Of course."

"You fucking guys..."

"Who's to stop him?."

"I guess. What else is going on?"

"Something strange…"

"When was it any different?"

Sebastian could not respond. Memories of fists, open hands and roaring crowds entered his head. He took the receiver away from his ear and pressed his temples with his hands. He heard Sheila's tinny voice calling to him.

"…What do you want with me?"

He re-clasped the instrument to his head.

"Go see him."

"Oh…"

"Don't tell him I called…," Sebastian said, and hung up.

She found Robin in a thick bathrobe, clutching a cup of coffee. His feet were perched against a table, his gaze fixed forward. The room was even more of a mess than usual.

Straight from the office, Sheila wore her business clothes and carried a briefcase and umbrella. She walked slowly about the room, picking her way among the clutter. She looked at Robin, smiling. "You even scared away your little brother…"

Robin looked sternly at her, took a drink of coffee and hand-worked his bruised jaw, wincing.

Sheila turned to look behind the couch, speared a pair of underwear with her umbrella and held it high.

"Tsk, tsk…"

Sebastian sat holding a beer can, hunched forward in a lawn chair on his parents' sundeck. His father sat where he always did, drinking a beer. Though it was not late in the day, the air was gloomy with a threat of rain.

"I don't know, Dad, you gotta figure...I'm gonna stay away for a while, let him think about it. He's a hell of a guy. Just screwed up right now, you know. Weird. At the same time they're giving him some kind of award. Best of something. Best History Teacher in The World, or something like that. You gotta know he'd either screw up totally or be the absolute best."

He stopped, slugging his beer. "You should be proud of him. You should. I should. Mom is, I'm sure. It's just that...I don't know."

In the silence, Sebastian breathed, then continued talking.

"Remember the radio? Remember that kid who delivered the paper stole my little twelve-transistor? Hah! What a mistake. Robin sees the kid one day riding around with it, comes home, gets some heavy gloves from the basement and says to me 'Wanna come get your radio?' I didn't know what he was talking about so I follow him down the street. He stops at the kid's gate and tells me to stay right there because they've got a bad dog. He gets a big stick from the ditch and goes on in, fights past the dog — that's what the heavy gloves were for — and knocks on the kid's door. The kid's folks aren't home but he knows what we're there for and hands over the radio. I've still got it somewhere. Robin fought that big dog. I was scared. I was watching and I was scared to death. He was swinging the stick and hitting it. It was a godawful bloody big Doberman or something like that. Big mouth, big teeth. I don't know how anybody could like one of those things, have it for a pet. I don't know, each to their own. I guess you could like it if you raised it from a pup.

"Robin started hitting as the dog ran up. It was fighting bravely. He hit it and hit it. I was watching him. I knew

I couldn't do anything like that. The dog got it in the eye and almost fell over. I yelled. They kept fighting. I yelled to him, 'Do you think this is right?'"

Sebastian rose, talking to himself, and walked around the sundeck. He mumbled, "Do you think this is right?"

4

Lena Josephine died a half-year later during harvest. Another cause for drinking and closer, more cruel silences. You lay fully clothed in bed in the afternoon. You could hear the boy going about his chores and voices in the downstairs room where candles were burning and Mama was laid out to look as best she could. You heard the pail for the hog feed. You brooded, wondering if the heat inside you was the whiskey or a cancer like the one that had burned the insides of Lena Josephine.

Respects paid, the neighbours made to leave. They spoke to the boy—you heard the voices but could not make out what was said. You heard their steps on the gravel. A car started, doors slammed. The motor drone died away. The sound of the feed pail again. You turned to the wall, closed your eyes and hoped for sleep. You could hear everything. Too much. Too goddamned much.

There was no more whiskey in the house. It went

before the neighbours arrived and the boy showed them in and they went about their condolences knowing that you, the man, had taken himself out of the business and was lying upstairs while his son worked. The last of the whiskey clung to the sides of the bottle and collected in a thin amber line at the bottom. It sat beside the bed where it was last plunked down by your unsteady hand. The sound of the bottle hitting the floor had echoed in the room and you cursed that the sound could certainly be heard down in the parlour. The sound never let up, echoed still in your head. All this sound. It never ended. It was because of the silence. The goddamn silence of this infernally flat, dead, ugly land.

You opened your eyes. The patterns on the wallpaper were still the same, the sounds in the yard, the light coming from the open window, all the same. The burning. Still there. You rubbed your eyes hard, trying to get the gloom out of them, rasping them red. You took your hands away and suffered the heavy heat at your face. Like hands pressing, hot and moist. It wouldn't go away, started to spread over your neck, your chest, your body. Hot, heavy hands pressing all over you, too hot, too hot...

You whipped the sheet away and sprang from the bed, clutching at your shirt, wet. You lurched down the stairs and through the parlour, past the dead woman, flung the door open and ran out across the yard and onto a field in your socks. You ran and ran, needing the fresh air on your face, until you were at the slough and though there were leeches and the fringes were mud and alkali, you stumbled down on your belly and buried your face in the water.

The boy, pail in hand, stood in the middle of the yard on the eve of his mother's funeral and watched.

You cleaned yourself up that night, shedding clothes in the barn and sponging off with a pail from the well. The water frigid cold, bitter. You shuddered, wiping your face, and struggled on a pair of breeches. On the way to the house you saw the boy coming in with the cows.

Indoors the heat of the day still held. You pulled a shirt on and stooped to find shoes. Your mind was clear at last, clear enough to take care of this farm. The boy did not know everything. You were the man.

Outside once again you remembered how, in this land, late summer brought grief to those who did not take care. The afternoon heat could drive you strange, but at night the frost came down just to be miserable to anyone who forgot to put a feather tick on the bed. You walked to the Model A and leaned against it, considering the brilliant evening sky. The radiator metal chilled a cold rut in your back. The boy came from the barn, chores done. You shivered, wishing you had a jacket.

"Boy."

"Yes, Papa."

The boy approached slowly and stopped a little way off. You did not notice his caution.

"Chores are done?"

"Yes, Papa."

"Cows…?"

"All done. Two buckets."

"Good."

In the gaps between his answers you noticed the silence and wished it were not there, though you knew who had built it so carefully. The boy was part of it now.

"Your mother…"

The boy's head bowed.

"Your mother…" The words were not there. You knew that if there was to be talk and instruction and control on this farm and in your lives you must get the words. Even speaking in the old language, you could not get the words. The boy kept the silence. Did he even know the old language? Could he hold it in there with the new one? What nonsense this was!

"She is to be buried tomorrow!"

The boy looked up, startled at your vehemence.

"We must be ready."

"Yes, Papa."

"Sweep the house. The porch. The neighbours must not see us living like pigs."

"No, Papa."

"Careful in the parlour. Don't raise dust on Mama."

"Yes, Papa…"

You gazed up at the blackening sky, trying to think. What else? Your head, you noted, now hurt. No whiskey in the house. No money. Some grain left in one of the silos but it would be at least until tomorrow afternoon that the funeral would be over and you and the boy could load up and go to town to sell the godforsaken stuff and get some supplies. Whiskey. The Model A's broad radiator again sent a cold shot through your guts. You shivered.

"Papa…? Are you well?"

"Eh?" Startled. You moved away from the car and looked around. Was there some cooking wine in the cupboards? She had kept the stuff up high so the boy might not fool with it. "Nothing…I am going to the house now."

"Lie down, Papa."

"I will. I will. Do your chores."

"Yes."

"You are a good boy." You put your hand on his fair head. Warmth. How is he so warm? It is freezing out here!

"Oh, another thing. Autumn is nearing. Take the water out of the car."

"The water?"

"It may freeze. Empty it. Fill it again in the morning. Just to be safe. We can't afford another car."

"Yes, Papa."

The boy worked until late and then emptied the radiator in the inky darkness, hearing but not seeing the fluid hissing in the dust. There were clouds and it did not look like it would get cold tonight as Father thought, but the boy knew orders were orders.

After washing in the barn the boy came to the house, fearing, as he climbed the stairs, the ranting in the kitchen.

In his bed, the boy could not shut out the awful sound from below. He couldn't push away the bad air of the room. Sleepless, he lay there for an hour, struggling. Then he rose, put on pants and shoes, snuck down the stairs past the kitchen and ran into the yard, out across the field where you had run earlier, past the slough and away.

When he got tired of running he walked, a long way, to the end of the field, feeling his way in the darkness across the rut-path and into the next field. He kicked at clumps of soil, wandered in circles for a while and sat down. He stared at the outline of his shoes, trying to see his own hand in front of his face. At times he thought he could hear barking — coyotes maybe, but slightly different. He strained beyond the rush of blood in his ears to hear more but couldn't. He quit trying, a soreness in his head. He looked back to the only beacon, the dim lantern light burning in the kitchen windows of the house, two fields away.

The question of what was happening, what was going to happen, what could make things better, never occurred to him. At the age of eleven, with his mother dead and you psychotic-drunk, I'm sure he had a practical grasp on things and knew the truth. The truth was that he was in for a rough time. The only thing solid to him was the way his rear end sat stone firm in the prairie soil that dark night.

He wandered in from the field and paused by the car to listen for you. He heard nothing. Good. At least there would be some sleep from now until the dawn. In the meantime, the car didn't have any water in the radiator and it was the kind of detail to get lost in the shuffle next day when the funeral started. Better to fill it up now so it wouldn't bother him trying to get to sleep. The clouds had held, keeping the ground-heat close. There wasn't the slightest chance of a freeze. The boy got a lantern, then water from the well, filled the radiator and slipped back upstairs past your loud snoring in the kitchen.

You woke up with the other kind of gut-shakes. The queasy-sick you get from rotgut wine instead of good, clean whiskey. The notion of vomiting presented itself, then passed. You rolled off the chair and hit the floor with your knees and hands. This was bad. Worse than usual. A man holds his liquor, does not act like a fool. Another wave of nausea clenched at your innards. You staggered to your feet and made for the door.

Coming back from the outhouse, a little steadier, you stopped to lean on the car and looked around. Dawn was about a half-hour off, the eastern skyline glowed faintly — the coldest part of the night. You shivered, holding onto the car, and it occurred to you to check the radiator. Not that you thought the boy might have forgotten. He was a good boy, good at chores, thoughtful and steady. A good boy, alright...

Goddamn it! The water was right up, cold as death to the touch, just about freezing sure as hell!

Scowling, you stooped to unscrew the plug.

On the way through the house, ready to whip some boy-ass for the insolence, the irresponsibility, the miserable negligence of it all, nausea hit again and stopped you in the parlour before Lena Josephine. You vomited on the floor, then slid to the couch, shivering, and passed solidly out of consciousness.

After the boy had cleaned the mess in the kitchen and the parlour floor, washed himself and put on Sunday clothes, the neighbours began to arrive and he had to shake you violently to wake you. He helped you into good clothes and went out to make tea for the ladies. When the hearse came, the boy and some of the men organised the pall bearing. He went back to your room and brought you down to the car. The neighbours clustered in hushed groups. The hearse driver stood by his vehicle, door open, foot on the running board, watching for instructions from the grieving family.

You looked around and smiled at the assembly.

A nod to the hearse driver. A neighbour slid behind the driver's seat of the Model A and another sat up front with him. The boy helped you into the back. At the first cough of the motor, your face darkened and you squeezed the boy's arm.

"The water."

"Yes, Papa. I got it."

"The water!"

"It's all right, Papa…"

"All right, all right…! The water!"

"I filled it this morning. You were sleeping."

The driving-neighbour turned, smiling meekly. "She runs fine," he said.

The road to church was a long climb to a mesa four miles from the farm, just about the only high ground anywhere in the district. Motoring the last mile the car started acting up, getting hot, but the slowness of the procession and the bumpiness of the road made it hard to judge if there was a problem or not. Still, when the cars had all turned into the churchyard and the Model A pulled up, the driver remarked to no one in particular, "She's workin' a little rough."

The service was short and the burial immediate; the plots were just a short pall-bear out back. As black soil thunked onto the casket, you woke up to something, bellowed, and stumbled against the boy standing close. The boy tried to quiet you, but you babbled and then, wild-eyed, grabbed his sleeve and proceeded to pull him out of the cemetery.

The neighbours parted a pathway as you ran to the car. The plots were close together, the parking area and Lena Josephine's grave separated by many tightly packed rows of settlers. On your way you trampled the graves. You and the boy made it to the car and you hit the starter. The boy knew there would be no reasoning with you. You left the funeral in angry dust.

You seemed upset by a number of things, but your flight from the churchyard was not motivated by the grief, confusion or delirium tremens you were suffering. You just wanted to get out of there. As you gunned the motor off the knoll and onto the main road, you knew, winding the revs as high as the Model A could manage, that this car could never take you fast enough, far enough, long enough away. The boy tensed and steadied himself against the door.

"Slowly, Father…"

"No!"

"Father…"

"Quiet!"

You made a turn by swinging wide and swerving, much too fast, down into the rut at the side, up over the crest of the road and into another rut on the far side of the turn. The car fishtailed and blew dust into the fields. The boy fought to keep a scream in his throat, braced himself even harder, feet planted on the dashboard to soften the impact he was sure was inevitable. You laughed, then caught yourself, bearing down with determination, gas pedal to the floor.

The car, now seriously overheating, began to make strange noises, and a burning smell permeated the front seat. You were impervious. The house came into sight, across two fields, and you impulsively jerked the car off the road, through the rut and onto a fallow field, bearing a straight course for home. The wheels sank low in the ploughed, dry ground, increasing the drag, making the car's demise that much more imminent; the motor roar now had a clanging to it, black smoke poured from under the cowling.

The boy, who had been fighting it for months, years now, began to cry. The tears came quickly in the smoke and wind, but even then he was glad there was so much sound no one, most of all himself, could hear the sobs.

As the car approached the highest point of the field, the

Model A's engine exploded. Fire took hold as the car rolled
forward. The boy knew death was upon him by the noise
and the lick of fatal heat at his tightly clenched eyelids. He
had stopped crying.

The car seized to a stop at the top of the rise, a fuming, heaving ruin. The boy opened his eyes. Such smoke!
Choking, acid smoke. This must be Hell! Eyes closed again,
he wondered if that was his father there beside him, clutching the steering wheel, staring ahead as if they were still
driving. The boy, gagging, then understood. He grabbed at
the door handle, found it, and was out on the prairie, running faster than ever, stumble-flying over the ploughed
rows in the fresh air. He tripped, ramming his face into the
dirt, his arms askew, hurting from the impact yet overjoyed
at being alive enough to hurt.

There was no hissing.

Sitting amidst the heat and fumes, you could hear
banging, the pinging of expansion and contraction, other
noises associated with extreme heat, but no hissing. That was
because, you realized, there was no water. No water in the
radiator. The car was dead now. The boy had killed the car.

The boy had seen something and was whooping, running off to the side of the field. The fire was ebbing,
staunched by lack of fuel and its own choking smoke. The
car sat like stone, deep in its ruts.

What the boy was whooping about, so soon after his brush
with The End, was a vision at the edge of the field toward
home: a dog.

Not just any dog. The boy couldn't mistake the outline, the way the head looked against the body, the sag of

the ears. As he got closer, he noticed the missing eye, the dishevelment, the twitch of the neck that hadn't been there before. Also the toothier grin, from loss of tissue around the mouth.

The boy accepted the Miracle of Maisie, because she looked like she had suffered so, and the boy knew about suffering. He was glad to see there could be a payoff.

With the passing of days — the funeral, emptying of silos, hauling the car off the field, buying supplies — the silence returned. You were not sure how you felt about this. The boy appeared to welcome it; he had his friend back and that did him fine. How to tell him about leaving, your intended flight to forget? And him boarding at the neighbour's farm for a while.

Harvest began, the boy worked and you drank whiskey and sometimes worked. On the porch one day, sitting, watching the boy and the dog bring in the cows, you wondered how you could ever have taken so many shots and missed. Impossible. Even drunk you knew you were better than that.

Fresh from a swig on the bottle, you raised the gun and sighted the distant bounding dog with speculation and wonder. Immortal dog. Live forever now. Got to admire her. Squeeze off a shot. A salute.

From two hundred and fifty metres out, with a slight wind, the bullet arrived a full second before the sound. The boy, warm with the fading autumn sun on his back, striding quickly along the trail, had his eyes on beautiful Maisie, wonderdog, as she raised her head in a bark at one of the reticent cows.

Wonder, as she rose strangely. Her front paws not jumping, but off the ground anyway. Did she yelp as the flat petting-spot between her ears exploded in red?

He can't remember now. It was a long time ago.

5

Robin's living room was back to being clean. Sebastian slouched on the couch, feet on the coffee table. He was bored, thumbing through a TV schedule.

Robin came in and plunked a newspaper down by Sebastian's feet. He was wearing his tweedy, history teacher work-clothes. "So, how's Mom and Dad?" he asked.

Sebastian looked up, then back to his magazine. "So now you care...?"

That evening, Sheila sat on the couch holding a near-empty wineglass. Sebastian entered the room.

"So...," said Sheila, "you're here for a few days."

"Yup."

"Baby-sitting big brother for a while..."

An awkward silence. Sebastian flopped into a chair and put his feet up. "I like you, Sheila. I've always liked you. In fact, maybe, in the darkest corner of my mind, I've liked you too much. Whatever. In any case, because Robin can't much fend for himself these days, and I need your help with him, I will do what I think best for all concerned and tell you, officially, without prejudice and with only the best interests of everyone in mind, to fuck right off. Nothing personal."

They stared at each other, grinning. Sheila laughed.

"You like me how much…?"

Robin came in holding a wineglass full of water. He strode to the couch and sat down.

Sebastian said: "I'm gonna open another bottle." He stood up. "Anybody gonna join me?"

Sheila smiled wider than she had before. Robin looked at his brother indifferently. "Bring it in. Somebody'll drink it."

"Right," said Sebastian, leaving.

"So…" Sheila drank her wine. "How are your parents?"

Robin sneered contemptuously. He drank. "S'not funny," he said.

"I know."

Sheila placed her glass carefully on the coffee table. "I hear you're getting that award."

"Uh huh…" He looked away from her.

"Still at it. Still teaching."

"Yup."

A pause. Sheila stared intently at him, then shook her head. "Still disgusted at just about everything."

"Maybe not everything."

"No?"

"You know it all, don't you?"

"No."

Another silence. They stared. Sheila retrieved her wineglass.

"Dad had a sister, you know," Robin said.

Sebastian returned, jovial, carrying glass in one hand, bottle in the other. "Let's put on some music!" he said.

Sheila spoke seriously to Robin: "No. I didn't know."

"Died as an infant."

Sebastian thumbed through some CDs. "How 'bout the Stones?"

"We're trying to talk."

"What about?"

"Dad's sister."

"Won't do any good."

"How do you know?"

"Nobody talks about it."

"So?"

"So…"

They glared at one another. Then Robin broke off, scowling, and drank water.

"I want slow music." said Sheila.

"What for?" snarled Robin.

"To dance."

"You're not here to dance. Remember that. You're not here to do anything but sign some papers, get your stuff and get out of here. You can thank Sebastian for dinner. It was his idea. You and he can still be friends. That doesn't concern me. I got a lot of other things on my mind, I don't want to go on and on about it. But you're not here to dance. Remember that."

Sebastian pressed a button and As Tears Go By began its dirgy mourning from the speakers. He sat on the couch beside Sheila.

"Robin…," Sheila said, "why be like this?"

"I can be how I want."

"Then don't talk to me about dead relatives!" She drank. "What should I care? Run after it all you want. Look in the mirror and cry. Dig up the remains. Look your father straight in the face and ask him. I bet you never do that…"

Robin barked, "Shut up!" then stormed from the room.

Sebastian and Sheila looked at each other and drank. Sheila sighed heavily. "Sorry." They listened to the sound of the back door, then a slam.

"Forget it. Same thing happened this morning."

"Oh?"

"Just read something in the paper out loud. All I did."

"He's been touchy. But now it's…manic."

"He's pretty calm usually."

"He's pretty sensitive."

"But, they're giving him that award."

"Apparently…" She paused, sipping wine. "Glad I'm not around."

He looked away from her, sipped his wine, then back. "I'm not," he said.

Sheila smiled, put down her glass, took his hand and pulled him up.

They smiled.

They danced.

They kissed, swaying.

Sheila gently broke off and walked to the window. She stopped, facing away from him. "He's so sad…"

The music mourned on.

The next day Sheila confronted Robin. He was distracted,

searching through the documents. She spoke, hands on hips. "We should have had a baby."

"You'd be holding it hostage by now."

"Her or him."

"Huh?"

"Her or him. Or them. Or whatever. Not 'it'."

"Ach...!"

Robin turned away.

Sheila said, "You're unattractive...Nowadays."

"I got women everywhere."

"That's not what I mean."

Robin scowled and went back to the documents. Sheila watched sadly for a time, then went to the couch and sat. Sebastian came in and sat next to her. They watched Robin.

"Get him some help," she said.

"Why do you think I'm here? Why do you think I called you again?"

"It's worse than that. He needs a professional."

"Aw, I don't know. What's wrong with him, other than a bad case of pack-rat-itis, or whatever it is that makes him keep all this old stuff and pore over it once in a while? I mean, what's wrong with that?"

"Don't play dumb, Seb. Not with me. We all know you're not. He needs you to take control or something..."

"Hmm... I'll take care of him, but...Well, he's the one that got himself this way, let him get himself out. He's always so smart. He's the one who helps other people. He never needs help. He always said that. He told me himself."

"Don't be silly..."

"I'll be what I want."

Sheila gazed for a silent moment at Sebastian. Then

she got up, walked, slowly at first, then with force, out the door. The back door slammed, and there was the sound of angry shoes pounding the wooden steps on the way down. He noticed that Robin was weeping.

Sebastian said: "Take it easy…"

"Where'd she go?"

"Where else? She's got some guy…Get a hold of your self, she's been gone for years. You'd think it wouldn't matter anymore. Anyway, to hell with her. You gotta get dressed."

"Phone 'em…Tell 'em I'm not showin' up."

"What…? It's an award for chrissakes. A trophy or a big plaque or something. What'll they do? Send it by mail? You gotta give a speech. Come on." Sebastian patted his brother on the back. "Where's your balls?"

"Forget it."

Robin turned away and sobbed across the table of documents. Sebastian sat back, considering. "I don't understand you," he said. "You're respected."

"I'm not going."

Sebastian got up and paced slowly about the room. He looked again at Robin quietly crying. He sighed and shook his head. Robin retreated to a hunched-over, face in hands, hiding posture.

"I guess you're not."

Sebastian left the room.

6

Robin fell off the couch.

Snuffling, he rolled onto his back, rubbed his nose, eased onto his side, snarled, and curled up. Twenty minutes later he opened his eyes, closed, opened them again, and focused. The binders, photo albums, pens and pencils strewn on the floor cut into his cheek. His high eye made out a heading he'd written in bold letters on a piece of notepaper.

REASONS.

He moved his legs, trying to stretch. His neck felt as if it might snap if he attempted to straighten. Finally he did and it didn't. In a minute he was on all fours, groaning, his housecoat bunched at the shoulders, buttocks bare to the prickly coldness of the room.

He stood, noticed himself in the mirror over the fireplace and staggered ahead to take a closer look. With elbows on the mantle, he slept again for a second and buckled to the floor, waking enough to know he was still too drunk and entirely too sad to wake fully. Then there was sleep and much motion behind his eyes, dreaming and distress. He drove endless roads, with pain in his body and his hands.

He finally awoke again, clenched and grunting, holding a coiling gut, and stumbled to the toilet. Washing his face, he wondered if it was a dream or a memory. His confusion concerned him greatly because it would not be good to lose one's sanity at quite this juncture. He reassured himself that this process, this disquiet, was indicative of a state of at least general mental health. Then he was lost in examining the red eyes weeping at him in the bathroom mirror.

A strange scar slanted across his cheek, painful to the touch. Robin's eyes blurred for a second; the look of the scar went abstract.

For a moment, it looked like a swastika.

He opened his eyes wide and rubbed the mark heavily with an open hand.

Barefoot over the mess — notebooks, photographs, albums — stubbing his toe on the portable typewriter he'd picked up in a flea market one summer-Sunday years ago in Bangor, Maine, Robin made it to the kitchen and opened the refrigerator door. The smell made him retch, almost toss his stomach, though he knew there would be little to toss.

He grabbed a half-empty bottle of mineral water, slammed the door shut to cut the odour, wrenched off the cap and chugged until he gagged.

Later, in the bath, Robin noticed the fine day outside. The sun shone through the old, wavy glass of the window, casting prism-flicker drawings on the water and on the wall. He sat up straight, making waves, and looked out. All was calm, familiar.

He blow-dried his hair and got some underwear. The clock radio flashed twelve o'clock, on and off. He set it to what time he thought it looked like: twelve-thirty. He pulled on jeans and a T-shirt and went outside.

The weather was nice, though autumn-cool. He knew once he got working it would be plenty warm enough. Wind wavered along the tops of the trees. Otherwise there were no sounds.

He walked to the end of the driveway. No traffic at all. He looked up and down his little stretch of country lane. Quiet everywhere.

A car appeared and startled him, roaring up from the far curve. He jumped back off the road, fearing it might be slowing down, but it charged on. He stood still, like a rabbit stunned in headlights, and listened to the sound fading. Eventually he marched back to the house, clear and decided.

Which car?

There were four: three sedans and a pickup; three of them Japanese, one European; all of them trashed.

One of Robin's early careers had been as the mechanic in a small garage where the sign 'Licensed Mechanic On Duty' is a fraud game. He'd gotten good, both at posing as a tradesman and, incidentally, at fixing cars. He surveyed the near-wrecks. The truck, although licensed and in better shape than the others, was out — he'd need more lock-up space than the cab could offer.

The Bug, probably. It was an early 1970's Super Beetle model with the rounded windscreen and 1600cc motor, good in its day.

He went back to the house, rummaged in a kitchen drawer for keys, found several sets, pocketed most of them, and returned to the cars. None of them was locked, but he needed the keys to open the hatchbacks to get two old tires out of one and a bale of wire from the other. Once the mess was cleared, Robin found that the seats in the Bug reclined just fine. The others stuck. Verdict: Volkswagen.

Now to get it running. The motor turned but didn't catch.

Robin pushed the car out of its ruts in the lawn and down the driveway to the garage. He stripped off the carburettor and found that to do a proper job he would have to clean off every other thing in the grimy engine compartment. The job turned hard and long. The day got warmer.

Toward evening, with engine parts bathing in gasoline and ignition parts spread out along the work bench, he went back to the house, cleaned the fridge of spoiled contents and made himself a sandwich with what was left. There was one beer in the last case of the pile of 2-4s stacked out on the back porch. He held it, stepped off the porch and shambled toward the woods back of the house.

With nothing in his mind he hurled the bottle as hard as he could into the bush. He heard it knock against wood but couldn't be sure it had broken.

Rebuilding the VW took Robin two days. He slept one night, worked through the other. When everything was done, he started her up, backed down the driveway and spun it up to eighty klicks per hour on his little stretch of road. She held together.

He drove back to the house, parked at the kitchen door and looked around at the trees, listening to the wind through them. It was dusk, the air held scents of warm earth, crops, farm smells. He thought once again of how he would miss this place. He went inside and scrounged something for dinner.

Robin had been happy — these last few busy, tiring days — not to think. As he munched a bowl of spaghetti covered with a glob of red sauce he'd found in the freezer, he realised he was thinking again. Voluntarily. He took this as a good sign.

He ran a hot bath and lay for hours with the window open, listening to crickets, sipping tea. He dozed, and started awake with the water frigid, teacup about to fall to the floor. He arose dripping and towelled off. The night was dark and silent; the crickets had quit, the wind was down. Robin walked through the house briskly, shivering.

He opened the sock drawer, fished around, and without conscious thought the packing began. He threw the two suitcases he had to his name on the bed and filled them with what clothes there were that were clean. He got just about everything that was needed into the tattered cases and the rest he stuffed into a green garbage bag. He pulled underwear out of one of the suitcases and put on a pair of jeans and a cotton T-shirt. He dragged the suitcases, garbage bag, a sleeping bag and two pillows off the bed into the hallway and left them by the door. Then to the living room...

By the fireplace there were a couple of cardboard boxes full of old newspapers. Robin dumped these upside down, splaying the papers over the hearth and covering some of the documents on the floor. With care he went to his knees and began sorting through the mess of papers, stacking photographs together, trying to organise some sort of priority; there was too much here to carry along. Resisting the compulsion to start reading and reviewing everything he put his hands on, he filled the boxes with what he thought essential, and dragged them to the mound of stuff by the door.

Outside, the air was turning morning-heavy, the slightest red tinge coloured the eastern sky above the trees. Robin loaded the car without care at first, and then deliberately when he found he couldn't fit as much in the space behind the rear seat as he'd thought.

In the kitchen, Robin threw the few cans and packages of food he had into an old cooler, made some orange juice and shoved that in too. The cooler was pretty well full. He chipped off several large chunks of ice from the over-frosted freezer, dumped them into a plastic bag, fitted it into the top of the crowded cooler and closed the lid.

It was day in the kitchen now, he flicked off the light.

His energy began to flag; he moved slowly, lugging the cooler out to the car. He was hungry and went back into the house. All he had left was a few pieces of bread and some cinnamon. He made coffee, toasted the bread in the oven and sprinkled on the cinnamon. He sat down at the table and munched the dry toast—the spice was just enough in the absence of butter or something sweet. The coffee was good, even without milk. Robin sat at the kitchen table and gazed at the beautiful morning it had turned out to be.

7

Because we lived so far away, and our family wasn't the travelling kind, the only time we spent with you was when I was young, pre-school and a little after when Dad got vacation at Easter. Maybe three or four days at your place every other year. You were the only person I knew who had a housekeeper. You wore lounging clothes all the time. But the thing I remember most, what sticks in my mind besides the cuff in the chops you gave me, was the rage in my father's voice, arguing with you.

We were used to hearing him yell, but never like he did with you. He might shout at us kids when we were bad, outside in the yard or playing on the street. But never inside a house, echoing off the walls. And you hollered back. Playing in the next room with toy tractors, I couldn't help but hear. I caught fragments. They didn't make sense to me then — I think you were talking about money, something I wasn't clear on in those days. I still don't know what it was about. I'm not sure if it matters now.

At other times you would just sit in your front room by the windows above the garden, sunning. Mom and Dad went out sometimes and left us with you. We played tentatively, not making much noise, threatened by the creakiness of your house, the alien-ness of your accent. Gave me the creeps. Looking up at you, I guess you gave me the creeps. Your face was thin and sometimes mean when you weren't smiling. You would watch us without expression. Sebastian was lucky, being younger, to maybe not feel the way I did. When you looked at the two of us with your granite face, I sensed you were only looking at me.

One time I got bored playing, and you gave me a project. We left Sebastian pushing trucks in the hall and went to the small room in the foyer where there was a closet with a heavy wooden door. "Go through these boxes," you said. "See if you can find something. There might be a toy in there."

I looked at the musty boxes and didn't like them, didn't like where they were, in a dark closet that smelled of old shoes and mothballs. Your voice was gruff. I wasn't used to a voice like that. Your hands were cold and thick-veined, what I imagined a dead person's would be like. When you leaned close, your breath sickened me. Decay. Not boozy though. Surprise — you'd quit, of all things. Stone swore off the stuff. I don't quite know what to make of that, I can only surmise that at some point after you got back, you saw Dad as he was, and tried to make another go of life; you saw it as your only chance.

To your credit, by god, you stayed off it. When I first met you, you'd apparently been bone-dry for nine years. Remarkable, when you think of the catastrophe-strewn trail of death and destruction behind you. All or most in the name of your need for the stuff, half the time — or maybe most of the time — I don't know. I'm not going to try to analyse this, only discover.

So there you were and your breath revolted me with its echo of greying meat and spongy floorboards. Dead cabins shut up all winter and wringing dank in the spring rains. You weren't an old man at that time, mid-fifties, but for me you were a haunted house. You laid your morgue-borne hand on my head and pointed my face to the closet.

"Little Robin. How good a detective are you?"

I didn't know what to say. You had the habit of not listening to what children said. Talking to me, you didn't seem to be looking at me so much as through me. Your voice was like that too. I'd heard other little kids on our street and in school who spoke of kindly grandparents, giving candy and taking them to the park. You always gave me the creeps.

There wasn't much choice for me at that moment so long ago, standing at the closet. It was my second trip to your house. You were supposed to be my super-wise grandfather. Misgivings or no, I didn't feel I had a choice. So I started digging as directed, with you standing there, and found to my surprise that it was enjoyable, picking through, discovering.

Old photos, hats and gloves, badges, letters and legal papers. A five-cent cigarette box that would be a collector's curio now. I almost forgot about you, standing there watching me.

The box that was deepest in the closet was almost as big as me; I had to pull it down on top of me. It was fun. This box, this biggest box, I clambered through, letting the papers fall over me, enjoying the buried sensation. I knew I could climb out. You must have been watching me closely, or maybe you'd left, I can't remember. But I know you were there when I found the cookie tin sealed with glue, impossible for me to open.

You were there, a paring knife in your hand, working the lid for a few seconds, grunting. Careful, I guess, to undo the stickiness without actually opening the lid. Leave it for me to discover. Make me an accomplice in knowledge, I suppose. You gave it back to me. The lid came away.

The only thing in the tin box was a little booklet. I was getting hungry, expecting cookies, and was disappointed. You knelt down beside me, put your hand over my hand, looked in my eyes and said, "Good, little Robin-bird. Good detective."

Your smile didn't warm me like Mom's did, or my friends' sometimes, but it was better than your frown or your gruffness. I could have reached out at that moment and touched your face. I could have touched you, or you could have touched me. Put your arm around me. As it was, your smile was a reward. I forgot about the box in my hand and wondered, with my young head, about you.

You took my hand with the book and lifted it to my face.

"See your Grandfather," you said. "See me."

I broke my gaze and fingered the book with both hands, flipping the little pages until I saw the photograph. A man with an even thinner face and a shadow of dark whiskers. In uniform. A sepia tone of black and white, faded and almost out of focus. There was a military-looking stamp partially obscuring the chin. I looked at you. Whitish, shining whiskers, but there was no mistaking. My first archival determination. Clear identification. I looked back at the photo. Funny writing below it. A stamp of something official on the opposite page. The man in the photo was not smiling, there was darkness under the eyes.

You were smiling. I smiled back. You pulled me up to stand before you. Without knowing why, I was proud. You patted my head, proud too, I could tell. We both stood there and felt proud. The photo in my hand was of a soldier, and I thought soldiers were just great, I'd seen lots of them on TV.

You stood there, proud, for a reason I don't know to this day. Beyond me completely. Maybe you hadn't quit booze early enough, brain-sizzled. Maybe looking at me you saw something of yourself, dare I say something good, and got that full, determined emotion fathers get. Beats the hell out of me. All I could think of was how good it was feeling proud. I suppose I was excited about discovering a new relationship in my life.

Anyway, later on you spoke to me at the dinner table like I was a little man, and Mom and Dad were surprised. You talked to me when the others were away, told me all the war stories. I was amazed at the detail, the wide world your stories described. It blew my mind. I was made privy to details of lives and deaths I would never have known, a world at war I would only have read about or seen on TV documentaries. You relished your task and did a damn fine job. You engendered my journey toward investigation and knowing. You told me most of your version of this very story. I loved it.

Then the next day, for some reason, Mom and Dad wanted to go out for a little while and they wanted to take you. They didn't want to take Sebastian and me but they didn't have anybody to leave us with.

You said: "Robin is a big boy. He will do."

Mom and Dad protested but you stuck with it. We looked at each other, respect shown and exchanged. My life was changed. I was ten feet tall. Mom and Dad finally shrugged their shoulders and wondered what had gone on between you and me.

You left me in charge. Sebastian played with his trucks, looked up as everyone went away; puzzled as a three-year-old gets, then indifferent, zooming across the dining room floor, making hills and roads out of folds in the carpet. I watched over him for a time, benevolent in my position as protector, in charge. A new role for me. Powerful but kind.

So I watched Sebastian and stood tall. Then I wondered what else I should be doing, other than watching. Sebastian looked up at me. We were both wondering. Then I thought it might be nice to do something together. Play a game or something.

Making a decision that was to affect both of us made me feel even more omnipotent. I crouched down to Sebastian's level and addressed him officially.

"Let's play tag," I said.

Then, considering, I rephrased: "We will play tag."

Sebastian's eyes brightened. He loved to play tag.

Taking his easy agreement as confirmation of my authority, I felt even more kindly toward the little kid. We'd always gotten along reasonably well, but from now on, I sensed, things would be different. Better. More ordered and respectful.

Sebastian, beaming, clambered up from the floor and toddled away from me, out of the dining room and toward the door in the sitting room. His route would follow a standard one: into the front hall, around to the big kitchen with its ancient, dreadful-dark appliances, a hard right through another door and back into the dining room. The circle route. We'd played it before, doing the wheelbarrow.

The game degenerated into a session of me following Sebastian and second-guessing his easily predicted movements. He laughed and bounced off the walls, scrambling to outwit me, surprised when I caught him by reversing direction and descending from nowhere. A panting, giddy happiness of play took us. We forgot ourselves, trying new things, crafting each other in different ways to flee and pursue.

We ran and ran. Bounced. Fell down, and ran again. Sebastian was getting winded, hysterical. His running got less and less efficient, until finally he stopped at one end of the route by the glass sitting-room door. I poised myself at the kitchen door and crouched in readiness. He laughed, falling over. I laughed too.

Sebastian collected himself and stood again. I could see his three-year-old's brain working something up. He looked at me slyly, then kicked the sitting-room door closed. The look on his face was that of a satisfied idiot, glad he'd done something even if not sure what. I was surprised and immediately desired to do a similar act of unguided defiance. I grabbed the propped-open kitchen door and swung it shut.

The sound it made, closing, made me start. I was happy to have done it — it got a laugh out of Sebastian — but the sound rattled me. The door had definitely clicked shut, steady. Something about it worried me. Sebastian laughed, a demented munchkin, holding his sides, struggling to stay standing.

I wanted to laugh, but couldn't. I went and tried the door. Locked, or stuck somehow, fast without any way for a kid to open it. I gagged, trying to hold on. I knew nothing of claustrophobia. I only knew I could not be held in a room, locked up. Unthinkable.

Sebastian was laughing at my actions: antics to him, meant to drive the comedy harder. He collapsed onto his bottom, guffawing out of control as I ran to the other door, the one he'd slammed, and wrenched at the knob.

You know what I was like when you and Mom and Dad came home. You must have been able to hear us from outside: Sebastian wailing in alarm, not knowing what was going on, sorely disappointed at the wild humour gone awry; me pulling at the doors in a raw panic I couldn't control.

Mom got the key and slid it under the glass door, trying to get me to listen and pick up the key and turn the lock. I was blind, beyond reason. All I knew was fear, the room had turned evil and dark. I was afraid I would die at any moment. I screamed and stamped around, senseless, flailing at dread's black hands gripping me from behind, squeezing my ribcage and making me suffocate.

The sight of familiar people behind the tinted, ornate panes of glass only made things worse. As my breath came in sobs, my heart weak and useless as rotten cabbage, I grabbed a heavy ashtray from an end table and ran it at the door.

The crashing of glass made Sebastian wail even more. Mom reached in, undid the lock, and then stood in the room not knowing which of her sons to comfort first. She picked up Seb fearing the worst inside his shorts. You marched into the room—I remember the crack and crunch of your shoes on the broken glass. I can see myself, standing there, weeping, rubbing my eyes. I knew you were there, looking at me.

You slapped me, hard, with an open palm. It made me punch myself in the eye with one of my balled, rubbing fists. The snap of it shocked my mother, standing with her back to us, and made me stop crying. I looked up, not seeing you, not seeing anything through the tears.

You slapped my face.

The sound of it echoes through me now.

No one had ever done it before, no one has since. I give it to you. It's yours.

It was the beginning of my adulthood, and here I sit now beside you.

8

The farm was rented, machinery stored, animals sold or slaughtered, and the dog conveniently dead. The boy, boarded at neighbours.

You're away.

I've seen the passenger manifest, even a faded old carbon of the ticket. There is no question of how you left. How you got back is a different story. I know most of it and I'll guess the rest. The ship was the Danish-registered *Queen of the Caucasus* out of Copenhagen. You got off in Amsterdam.

Then southeast overland, I don't know exactly how, mostly by train. It took maybe a week and you arrived sometime around the first part of December. Fifteen years had made slight difference in the place — you were surprised how little, pleased, in fact. Things were the same: solid.

The relatives were surprised to see you. They treated you suitably, as one who had recently lost a wife. No work for now. No bother at all. It was good to speak the language. It was good to drink homemade wine, though you missed the quick hit of whiskey. You remembered how poor it was here, no whiskey.

Nevertheless, it was good for the first while. The winter was not as cold. People were around, folks you could relax with. It was well into the new year, February, before anybody wondered what was next.

Old Uncle Agon, never your favourite, hadn't said much, but one day took you aside and put the question: "What are you doing?"

About the farm. Your boy.

"When are you going back?"

"Soon," you said. Things to do, spring seeding to see to, machines to rebuild. "Soon I will leave."

But you knew in your heart you needed more time, hadn't even started wanting to go back, felt like you might never feel that way. And then there were the women.

You had an interest again. Maybe it was the abstinence from hard booze, maybe the easy way the women acted their place in the old country. You dallied as much as a man can without being too obvious, and then one day at a family gathering you met Tasha. She was beautiful, smart, polite, maybe all you ever wanted in a woman. Never mind that she was your cousin's wife. Yantz was a distant cousin, it's true. But Tasha was his wife.

You forced yourself on her at a picnic outside the village, a place where you could walk alone in the trees and lie out by streams without too much chance of being seen. You had a force wrought from craziness and knowledge of the edge of life. You were back from there, did she know? She fought against you, but not too much — she'd seen you looking at her. She knew it was pointless to resist. She knew it would be worked out between the men, you and Yantz, sooner or later. She might have been pretty and sharp-witted, but she was still a peasant in a country suspended in the quaint totalitarian traditions of paternalism.

Tasha was good at keeping secret the intimate clues that pop out of affairs of the heart and groin. Apparently, she did not drop a clue to Yantz. You saw little of the man and arranged your visits to her village to coincide with Yantz's long working hours in the fields far away. Soon everyone knew but him. The village cronies, collected at the square, knew where you were going, though few knew who you were.

This affair, dragging through April and May, irritated Uncle Agon. "What are you doing?"

"Nothing."

"Damn you," said Uncle Agon.

The family became cool after that; you were encouraged to take a small place on the edge of the village and told to help anyone whose farm needed helping. You worked half-heartedly and ended up living on your dwindling but relatively valuable foreign currency. Every few weeks you took a trip into the city to the exchange. It appears no one outside the family saw the Canadian cash you carried. No one informed on you.

The affair with Tasha continued until September. By then you were starting to feel the need to go back; enough of this old-country stuffiness; you were surprised to be missing the wide sky. It got to be September, in the year 1939.

You were too busy consorting with your mistress and guzzling wine to notice that there was heaviness in the land. You didn't take much interest until the day Uncle Agon and the others came to you.

"What are you going to do?"

"What about?"

"Don't be foolish…"

This was unexpected and they'd picked their time wrong, too. You were in the middle of a wine-soak, deeper than usual, and your head was having trouble decoding tough concepts.

But it was true. It was now dangerous in this, your former homeland, to be foreign.

Foreign. Must have sounded bad to even speak the word. Especially in those times: dark, Gothic, just a musty history-tunnel to me, but for you, well, I'll leave it at that. Uncle Agon had a plan.

Yantz had been conscripted; no word on when he'd be back, if ever. Why didn't you go and live with your whore, that Tasha-slut that nobody wanted to talk to anymore? This village was too hot for you to stay in. People suspected or knew your status. Over there, nobody seemed to know. You'd have a better chance.

Against what? You wondered.

The wine was having a deep and tragic effect.

This thing was getting out of hand. Living openly with a woman who wasn't your wife? You were a drunk, sure. You'd done crazy things, cruel things. But somewhere deep down you had this strange, Victorian-esque morality. Anyway, the decision was made for you. The family, saving their own asses, evicted you from the shack. They grabbed your passport and burned it. You had to go.

Soon there was a quick rush of military through those parts — everywhere you looked — then martial law. You couldn't wander to the city anymore, restricted travel. Everybody was suspicious of everybody else. But you survived through the efforts of Tasha. She was good with the neighbours, good at keeping the questions benign and easing you into her life as if you'd always been her husband. People even started calling you Yantz.

Things settled down as much as possible under the circumstances. You worked some of Yantz's old jobs. Tasha's two children slowly came to accept you. By the next spring she was carrying one of your own. Everything looked rosy enough, despite the military presence, until harvest, when trucks rumbled into the square and the announcement was made that eighty percent of everything was being taken. The young men scowled and spit on the ground; mothers gripped their children closer; the old folks wailed, pitiful, like farm animals. You were revolted by their crying. You found it easy to stay calm. This was not your land, no longer your people. The place had become more and more pathetic to you as time went on, petty emotions about petty land that had lost its future long ago. This place was dead. Your instinct was to flee.

Harvest was performed under guard. Every bushel was counted. Every ham, every egg. It was amazing to see how everyone adjusted to living on twenty percent of what they had before. People went lean before your eyes, you could see them shrink and wrinkle. The military commander of the district seized the seed grain and held it in a communal silo for distribution the next year. Heavy guard was posted on feed for livestock.

How could you get out of here?

Your little daughter was born close to Christmas. I

searched long and hard, the records are all but gone; I couldn't find the name you gave her, if any. It probably didn't feel much like Christmas.

Particularly because of the lack of booze. The grape crop had been seized outright and taken away for sugar production. You were in deep shit, alcohol-wise. There was nothing to work with, only enough potatoes and grain to keep the family fed over the winter. Everything was rationed out on a daily basis. You were strapped.

So the winter passed slowly. You must have been a devil to live with, but at least Tasha had a new baby and the concerns of keeping home and family together in starvation conditions to divert her. You mumbled to yourself a lot and kept close to the kitchen fire.

The next spring the work was different: drudgery, people not liking this life or each other. There were still more military, though not so many doing guard work. Rumours started about the fighting coming nearer. No one knew anything for sure. A special kind of military set up shop in the village. Word went out that they were kidnapping people, making them disappear. But you weren't concerned, busy as you were trying to figure out how to get some booze happening.

Nor did you care what a bootleg operation might cost your family. You got in trouble that year when the local commandant found out the civilian food supply was being pilfered. Somehow this stuff got swiped and stored somewhere and you collected enough pots, pans and hosing to make a personal distillery.

By October, moonshine production was under way. Drunken soldiers started turning up on guard duty. This got the commandant in a wicked snit and he took measures. Who knows how many others got it; anybody wrong-place wrong-time got scooped; searches were total. You were in the woods foraging fuel for the still when they came to Tasha's house. She and the children were taken away and nobody knows what happened to them. They didn't turn up anywhere after the war.

You were on the edge of town with a price on your head, your existence more tenuous than ever before. You started running. Running at that time and under those conditions was difficult, you must have had assistance. God help those people. I hope at least some of them survived. You travelled through wartime countryside with no paperwork, no legal status. Capture, imprisonment, maybe torture and death should only have been a matter of time. Did you know how dangerous it was? You lit out toward the east and got lucky and they still haven't caught you.

The scenery was like northern Saskatchewan if you blurred your eyes and forgot about the language. The weather was crisp with winter coming on. By keeping off roads, away from checkpoints and patrols, you stayed on the loose, and came upon the occasional fish pond or rabbit snare. You ate what you could find and slept in barns. Starved for a drink.

One day the rabbit supply was low, it was raining and the sullen sky told you snow was close. A village popped out of the hills and you could see from high ground a line-up of men dressed in warm work clothes. They stood in the square and rubbed their hands, breath visible in the chill. There were no soldiers around and you could sense by the way they stood and the occasional puff of steam rising from a doorway that the men were lined up for food. You could almost pick up the aroma, and you knew this was it, time to try the bold route for a change.

On the edge of the village, parked in ranks by a rutted field, were a dozen trucks. A soldier barked something harsh, but you kept on as if you knew where you were going. You could smell the food. You joined the end of the line. It was surprising how well you fit into the rabble. No one looked at you with much curiosity. A few other men joined the line behind you and seemed just as new. You spoke to them. Some of them spoke your language, others spoke other languages. The food, served in a mess hall that had once been a church, was life given back to you.

Full, you looked up to notice that the few soldiers standing around held their weapons at rest, not pointing, not guarding. The men seemed to have freedom of movement. This might not be so bad. But the man next to you who spoke your language, and others nearby that you could see, looked about with sorry eyes.

After the meal you followed the general movement, in clumps and small groups, out of the square toward the truck convoy. Without direction or signal, the men drifted up onto the wooden benches in the covered trucks, waiting and smoking.

You found a place nobody seemed to be using. The trucks started. The convoy rolled eastward. If you'd been paying attention back there instead of drinking and lolling around, you'd have known that the war was in this direction, at least the biggest part of the war. In two days the convoy was deep in the Ukraine.

It was all the same to you. The food kept up, though the farther eastward the poorer the quality. You discovered you were in a work party going to the active areas to repair bridges and build barracks. Somebody asked where you were from and your nod to the west, your: "Back there," got a laugh from everybody. You made a point of speaking little to anyone. You obeyed orders wordlessly. Then one day they ordered you all off the trucks and drove away. They left a mobile kitchen. You worked in a gang of tree cutters, hewing and clearing, cutting boards, building crude barracks. The snow came before you finished. There was much work during this time. You lost yourself in it, the only thing to do in a prison without bars. No homeland, no liquor, farther from home than you dared tell anyone, and not even a fake identity to lean on. You told them your name was Yantz.

One day the next spring you were sent out with others to repair a bridge that had been bombed. Up until then you hadn't seen anything that looked like war, but here were rent timbers, burned planks and craters you could park a motorcycle in. Airplanes passed high overhead as you worked. On the third day, almost finished, the sound of airplanes came closer than usual, lower, but no one paid attention. A bomb struck the bank of the river; the men looked each other in the eyes. A soldier, standing on the bank, ran for cover.

Another bomb hit the bridge deck and threw a timber wobbling your way. In slow motion, it hit the man next to you and separated his body neatly in the middle. The face and chest spiralled away from you with the wood, spinning in the air. There was just you — too shocked to duck — and half a body, standing on the bridge. When the next bomb hit, it sent you and the parts flying over, down, into the water.

The current was strong. You surfaced away from the

bridge and floated down river, landing on the muddy bank. You heaved, dry, nothing came up. The shock wore off and the coldness penetrated, killing you, you knew clear as the water lapping over your feet. You looked at the legs beached beside you. Ragged viscera hung about, but you were struck by how natural the rest of it looked, like you could reattach the top, if it could be found, and the man would get up and brush himself off, cursing the close call. You could not get your eyes to look away. Something gnawed in your mind, there was more you should be doing here, you knew, than just gawking. Moments ago, this fellow had been like you, working away. Same height, weight, age, even eyes and hair. The man's belt and pockets were intact, a margin of paper poked out of a back slip pouch. You reached and drew the paper out — identification.

The others came and picked you up, carried you to the truck and back to camp. It took hours in front of a red-glowing stove to thaw out, your fists clenched so tight you couldn't hold eating utensils. Alone in your bunk you eased your fingers open and hid the papers under the mattress.

The season became warmer and then it was hot. The work continued and you were moved around all over the place, building, repairing. The food got bad and scarce. Supplies dwindled, until you were working with broken, blunted tools, fixing shattered buildings with shattered boards, bent nails. Then it was winter again and you froze, no fuel for the barrack stove. Men died that year for the first time of the cold, lack of food, loneliness. The work kept up.

Then there was talk of moving back, west, away from the war. The talk speculated that the war was coming close, things were going badly: Russians were advancing.

You didn't know. By now you were in a fog so thick

you almost forgot your name wasn't the one on your stolen I.D. You'd forgotten about relatives in the old country or Tasha's soft advances, or even about Canada and a place back there that was still legally your own. Or a son.

The weather was a thing of evil darkness, cruel in its death-dealing. Survival would soon be a casual impossibility. And worse, you thought you heard bombing sounds, particularly at night. The war? The image of a man cut apart did not leave you. Your faith in a future rested only on the hope, the belief, that someday you might once again taste the sting that whiskey made on your tongue.

9

The harshness, the proximity of an engine sound, a full roaring thing made by an American four-wheel-drive truck breaking the peace of the morning told Robin he'd been dozing at the table. The bit of coffee left in his cup was ice-cold. Footsteps crunched around the house to the kitchen door.

"W'lenco? W'lenco, you home?" Robin heard in his landlord's voice the wild bush resonance of a hundred tailgate beers drunk in the company of a few good men. Boots thumped on the porch, knuckles clunked against the door. The fuzzy outline of a country youth showed in the screen.

"Come in, Randy. Door's open."

"W'lenco?" He pushed open the door and leaned in. "You goin' somewhere?"

"Just some things I'm throwing out. Didn't you see the garbage bag?"

"There's suitcases too. You owe me money, W'lenco."

Randy stood in his heavy boots, staring ferociously. Robin had known this was coming, but he'd forgotten. All he could think of this morning was how perfectly Randy's harsh voice fit with his rumbly truck.

"Ain't you s'posed to be at school?"

Robin wondered if Randy knew just how heavy and difficult that question was. Probably not.

"Uh…Professional day. I'm off."

"Jeez, you teachers got it slack. When you get paid next?"

Another tough question, hanging like spoiled air in a sealed room. The quiet and peace outside was tangible, but too far away.

"I don't think that's any of your business."

"When?"

"Soon."

"You got a week."

"Fine."

"…Seven days."

"You'll get it."

"I better."

The rumble of the truck died slowly. Robin finished his toast.

The return of silence and whispering trees was not comfortable. The thing to do immediately, the instinct down in his bones, was go.

Go now.

Robin threw the frigid coffee in the sink. He rinsed the dishes and executed the final phases of packing.

He wrapped a few dishes and utensils in tea towels and dropped them into the car on the way to the garage.

The smallest of the toolboxes was full of odds and ends, nails and screws, rusty and useless. He dumped the mess into an old railroad tar barrel and made himself take the time to choose carefully from the workbench and other boxes those tools that he would haul along.

It was mid-morning when he tucked the heavily loaded box in among the other goods in the car.

He went back to the house for the last time.

In the bedroom, he forced open the closet door against some debris on the floor; the junk wedged hard up against the bed as he forced his way in. He squeezed into the space, pulled the lightstring and struggled for a box on the overhead shelf. Robin reached into it and rummaged past thick envelopes full of photographs and papers. His fingers touched cool metal, a memory of Boy Scouts, a solid, powder-smelling flashback of holding, loading, aiming, shooting...Robin's ancient, single shot, bolt action .22 calibre target pistol was once again in hand.

His motivations present, a stone-solid fact in his mind, he held the weapon firm and could not stop himself from uttering out loud: "Fuckin' A."

With the box teetering on one hand, the other holding the gun, Robin peered in to see if there were any bullets. He stuck the weapon in the waistband of his jeans, trying to ignore the movie-violent image this created in his head, and shook the box. With his free hand he located some capsules rolling around among the love letters and out-of-focus instamatic images of camp, recreation and the past. He found eleven rounds.

Back outside, Robin inspected the interior of the car, then upended the back seat, sticking his hand into wires, sharp objects and metal. There was a good hiding place if he cut the upholstery and shoved some insulation out of the way.

He struggled, sweating, and duct-taped the gun up into the seat, then rolled the bullets in tape and fastened them in beside the gun.

The VW started like a new car even though it had 157,000 klicks on the speedometer. Robin drove in a circle on the lawn and paused to take a last look at the house. A nagging detail tugged at him, made him hesitate to leave. Remembering, Robin cut the engine, got out and rummaged for a screwdriver. He removed the license plate on the truck and transferred it to the VW.

Confident that all was done, Robin fired up the motor and pulled quickly down the drive, turned at the road and was gone from the place.

On the ride to town, Robin tried to think of all that he had to do. First, there was the question of money.

It looked to be around two in the afternoon as Robin motored down the quiet main street and stopped in front of the bank machine.

His card slid in nicely. He punched in his personal identity number and jabbed instructions for a chequing account balance. It took a second, then flashed: $310.73…

What!

He leafed through his wallet for the withdrawal cards he kept to save him from having to maintain a chequebook. He couldn't find anything later than ten days ago when there had been almost nineteen hundred dollars.

He jabbed instructions to check his savings balance.

$15.35. Where once he was sure he'd had at least a thousand. Disappointing to be sure, but not a big surprise.

He told the machine to give him the $310 from his chequing. He tried to think while it whirred and dealt. Then he extracted the ten-dollar minimum accessible from the other account. In the car, he held his head in his hands and tried not to obsess about where the money might have gone. Not only that, it had been months since he knew exactly how loaded his credit cards were. He was afraid to find out.

Robin was used to the phantom-alcoholic disappearances of surprising sums of money. This was the past; he knew it well. What he did not know well was how he would do what he wanted to do on a fraction of the required cash. Minutes ticked by. Robin watched people wander up and down the street.

He was impressed by how empty his mind was. After a while he forced himself to think about something. It came to him that the nature of this void presently in his head was somewhat like the empty space he was seeking to fill by undertaking this trip. He became aware of the passage of time and the hum like radio static of the village life around him. He touched the ignition key and the car seemed to start itself. He rolled away from the curb and down the road.

At the first service station with a knickknack store, he got a fill-up and pulled out his North America Road Atlas. A picture of an open road was on the cover, with impressionistic scenes along the way: forest, desert, waterside and city. It transmitted freedom, with its easy-to-decipher mileage tables, its index of camp spots and national parks. It had big maps, with all the Canada-USA-Mexico major highways and cities displayed in their complicated linkages. It had individual state and provincial maps, all the little roads you could take to any place you cared to go. The weight of it in his hands gave Robin an odd confidence.

He made the ferry in forty minutes, experiencing the usual twinges on leaving beloved Vancouver Island. On the mainland he drove as hard as he could to the Trans-Canada and then, for as long as his eyes held out, down the long, twisting Hope-Princeton Highway. With the passing of distance and time, the fatigue in his bones, Robin realized he wouldn't be making the kind of all-day-all-night, drive-like-a-madman-and-get-there-in-three-days run for it that he'd visualised.

At a diner he ate a hamburger and pored over the maps, debating which border crossing to go for.

Not long after, driving again, he got sleepy. The tough days of overhauling the car, stripping the house, leaving town, worrying and thinking, had wasted him. Still, he did not want to stop, forcing himself to drive further in the darkness.

Right-side wheels dragged dust, the steering wheel bucked, and Robin realised he'd drifted off at the wheel. He got control, blinking painfully in the oncoming glare of headlights, and pulled over at a small riverside park. He drove down an unlit treed lane to a secluded parking lot and switched off the engine. Then he crawled into the passenger seat, reclined it all the way back and bundled himself in the sleeping bag.

He did not sleep immediately. The dark spooked him. The drone of heavy trucks a half-kilometre away on the highway kept him thinking. In the end he faded, and woke to the murky light of early morning. It was raining.

He opened the passenger door, rolled out of his sleeping bag and walked to the back of the car, unzipping his fly. Taking a long, easy piss, steam rising from a frothy puddle in the mud, he knew for the first time since the summer got old the tinge of cold around his ribs and on his back. Just as well to be heading south. The murk amidst the trees and thick forest hung solid, un-moving, deadly silent. Not even the occasional rumble of a truck anymore.

Then above the hiss of his stream Robin heard a low vibration through the trees. The volume steadily grew and then another sound made it unmistakable. There was a train rolling somewhere off in the woods. He looked around. Probably a freight, going slow, by the lowness of the sound, and climbing a hill or something. A long one with heavy cargo.

Trains.

The rumble sounded like death. He thought of the Vietnam war, the one he'd watched on television; there were no trains in that one. It had helicopters; they sounded like this train did now. As a kid in the 1950s, Robin had watched helicopters with fascination and delight. The passing years did not dampen this ebullience but the television war certainly added a few elements. Who could deny the image-power of the deadly Cavalry helicopters, bristling with guns, kicking up dust and blood for the cameras?

Still urinating, Robin daydreamed back to a day in the early 1970s, swimming off Wreck Beach. Naked people all around, a hot afternoon and lots of red skin. Robin swam out about a hundred metres and floated on his back, alone, bobbing with the driftwood. The vibration was something he'd sensed as much as heard. He sensed the heavy beating and the secondary bouncing of concussions on the ground below the low-flying bird. A Cobra gunship, in all its television-famous Gothic menacing, swung from behind a near point and was instantly above Robin and the naked bathing

public. Grinning army crew-cuts eyeballed the nude frol-
icking women. Robin saw the swivel tracks and gun
carriage mounted inside the door, a stark vision of what
was being handed out to ground-bound people in other
parts of the world. The air pounded like hand-slaps on his
face; the airborne boys, smiling their horny naturalness,
spread dread with their presence and their nasty vehicle.

Trains seemed a relatively innocent weapon. Most
people didn't identify the possibility of a train being used for
anything other than transportation. But Robin Wallenco
knew that trains had been used to kill more humans than all
the helicopters built so far. But these trains, rumbling by on
this British Columbia morning in September, probably carried
nothing more suffer-bound than grain and pick-up trucks.

Robin zipped up, shivering, and drove the car out of
the forest.

First of all it was south on 21 for the crossing at Porthill,
Idaho. Then the border check and a stop to change money.
After ten miles of state highway — friendly enough terri-
tory — Robin wanted to turn back. The road-scares were
getting to him. Inexplicable shivers rippled down his back.
The occasional cold sweat. Though prepared for it, this was
worse than he expected, worse than ever before. He wondered if he'd finally wrecked his health with the drinking.
Doubts, anxieties, more shivers and then a black depression dogged him. He was angry that his purpose out here
on the road was not strong enough to fend off these pesky
psychological phenomena. Loneliness set in and he knew
he wouldn't last long.

He saw a hitchhiker.

As Robin got closer he didn't like the look of the man:

husky, with a hint of wildness in the face. Amazing how much he could sense, just a flash by and a pinpoint look in the eyes.

The next was a woman. She was tough-dressed but intelligent-looking; young; packsack, heavy shoes; a professional wayfarer, by the look of things. Robin studied and slowed down. He sensed her checking him out quickly, with practised, scanning eyes. He stopped the car. She finished looking at him, then jumped in, smiling.

Robin gunned the car back onto the highway and didn't realise he had forgotten to ask "Where you headed?" until third gear.

"Nowhere. Everywhere."

There was a twang. Midwest.

"Okay..." He hoped for some friendly elaboration. Nothing. He looked at her again. With one eye on the road he saw a tattoo, something like a serpent creeping up her neck. And she was younger than he thought. Much younger. First mistake.

"How old are you?"

"Seventeen."

"Really?"

"How 'bout you?"

"Huh?"

"How old are you?"

"Older than you."

"You're not being very nice..."

Her voice had a self-calm about it that made his heart slow down. He looked away and up the road, thinking, uncomfortable.

"Sorry. I'm thirty-eight."

"Whoa, gross! That's old!"

"Hey…"

"Don't be so serious. I didn't mean it."

"I'm glad."

"What do you do for a living?"

"I teach school."

Her face firmed with thought. She looked around at the country landscape rolling by. "What day is this?" she asked.

"God, I don't know. Haven't been keeping track."

She went into a zipper pocket and searched, fiddled, fingered, until she found a small book.

"September fourteenth," she said, flipping pages.

"Is that so?"

"Shouldn't you be in school?"

He turned from his driving. "Shouldn't you?"

"I asked first."

"This is my car, I make the rules."

"Okay. I'm a dropout. How 'bout you?"

"I like the sound of that. I guess I could call myself a dropout, too. If I wanted to."

"Your car. You make the rules."

Fifty miles later he had her name: Norma. It took another stretch of highway to get her home state: Arizona.

"How long you been on the road?"

"Eight months."

No elaboration. Next question.

In her presence Robin found himself inarticulate, and struggled with the impulse to just come right out and ask her the blunt questions on his mind. He wondered how far she would ride with him.

"So, really now, where are you headed? I mean, I'm going southeast, generally."

"That's fine."

"But how far?"

"How far you going?"

"Pretty far. All the way."

"All the way. That's pretty far. You mean Florida?"

"Not really. Somewhere in the South. Virginia, for sure. Other places maybe. I'm not too sure on details."

"That's fine."

"No it's not fine. I mean, surely you've got some place to go."

"Yes. But I'm not going there right now."

"Oh…"

"Why don't we just leave it for awhile. You can drop me off if I bother you."

"No, no, it's not that…"

"Then let's enjoy the ride. Are you tired? Would you like me to drive?"

"No, no. I'm ready for something to eat, though."

They stopped at a diner and ordered burgers. Norma breezily initiated a conversation with the waitress. Her friendliness was infectious. Robin caught himself smiling at something she said and realized he had almost forgotten who he was for a moment, what he was doing.

He had an uneasy moment, going back to the car, when he thought she might gather her packsack and say a cheery good luck, change direction. But without hesitation she took her place in the passenger seat, buckling up like she meant to stay.

Two hundred miles later, outside Butte, Montana, they pulled off the Interstate and drove to a private campsite he had got her to find in his five-year-old issue of *Camping on the Road in America*. The place was barely operating, the season virtually over, and they were directed to a vast wooded area they had all to themselves.

Norma hopped from the car and looked around, pleased. "Better than I'm used to."

"Well, I'm gonna need a shower."

"You don't smell so bad."

"Yet."

"Oh."

"Anyway, you can sleep in my tent if you want. I'll sack out in the car."

"Fine."

"Good. I'll set up."

"What can I do?"

"Maybe check if there's a store around. Get us some groceries."

Robin handed her a twenty-dollar bill. Norma took it and tucked it in her shirt pocket. "Any preferences?"

"I dunno. Get us a couple of steaks or something. I got some canned stuff in the car. Vegetables. Just fill in the rest. Something easy."

"Okay."

She marched smartly off.

Immediately her absence left a cold hole in him, a hostile space, full of knowing that he had been conned. Then he saw the packsack and damned himself for thinking that way.

He set up camp, beginning to feel like he was on the road for real at last, the second night out and a travel companion to boot. Norma trudged up the lane with a bag in her arms.

"This is a cute place," she said, plunking the bag on the picnic table.

"Desolate and forlorn, maybe. Don't know if I'd ever call it cute. What did you get us?"

"Barbecued chicken. Ready-cooked."

"Great!"

"Some apples for dessert."

"Fine."

"Have one of these."

Norma fished in the bag and came up with a six-pack of beer. She tossed him a can. He caught it, stationary, looking awkward.

"God, this'll taste good." She pulled a can off for herself and pulled the tab. "Cheers." She drank, then sat herself on the table and looked over his work. "Nice tent."

"Yeah. Thanks. I don't need this."

Robin put the can on the table and turned to his job. He gathered the little bag the pegs came in and got his hatchet from the ground. "How 'bout a fire?"

"Great."

He began to chop kindling. He could sense her watching him, sipping her beer. He was not surprised when she said: "Did I do something wrong?"

"No."

"Not your brand or...?"

"I don't drink. Or shouldn't. However you like."

"Oh."

"It's no big deal."

"Okay."

He kept working, hoping that was the end of it, knowing her eyes were on him. He turned to her.

"It's not a big deal."

"You said that, but look, here's your change back. I'll get the beer. We'll split the food."

"Forget about it."

"No, no. I'll pay my way."

"Sure you will, but forget about the beer thing. You didn't make a mistake. I appreciate the thought."

"Okay."

"Okay." She smiled, touching his arm.

He turned away, fiddling with the tools, putting things away in the tent bag. He tried not to experience the thrill of her touch. This was something he hadn't figured on dealing with for a while yet. Maybe when all this business was finished but not before. He felt himself losing it, his resolve, and tried not to enjoy the tightening in his crotch. He turned to her again. Her smile was real. He sat down, sighed and chuckled casually, rubbing his head in his hands.

They sat, eating the chicken and then the fruit. It got dark. Norma yawned and said she was tired. Robin said he was tired too. But something more than fatigue was bothering him; he hoped it didn't show. There was pressure. In his head, in his chest. It was getting worse.

Norma went away to the washrooms with her towel and toothbrush, came back and said goodnight.

Robin had to grip the bench with both hands to steady himself.

Norma squirmed her way into the tent and struggled out of her clothes. In the dark she was a black blob, undulating.

Robin got up, unsteady, trying to think of something else. The salty taste of the chicken in his mouth. The dark, peaceful quiet of this place.

Beautiful.

He picked up Norma's half-gone can of beer. It wasn't

cold anymore. More like room temperature. The scent of spoiled vegetables was there, the barroom smell, the luring alcoholic tint on the air.

This was almost too much for him to take.

Robin poured the beer onto the gravel. The fire flickered in the background. Strength flowed out of him. The noise of movement from the tent had stopped. The pouring beer sounded like piss hitting the ground.

He shook the can out, trying for every drop. He shook harder, squeezing, desperate.

A remembrance of taste.

Almost self-saved, Robin stuck the crumpled can to his mouth.

One drop.

Just a taste.

Robin thrashed ahead, bent and dumbly determined, bulling his way through the woods. Darkness was no deterrent to him as shrubs fell, snapping back in his wake.

He entered the road, saw lights over a doorway and a neon beer sign, and plodded on. Inside the store he stood fully erect a moment, composing himself. There were a couple of kids buying candy and the man tending the place, nobody else. The beer was in back. At the counter he plunked a six-pack down and saw bottles behind the storekeeper.

"And...gimme a pint of bourbon, willya?"

"This kind?"

"No, the other one."

"One Jack Daniels."

The items sat on the counter between the two men.

The storekeeper, a bespectacled man of retirement age, predictably country, peered at Robin.

"That be all?"

"Uh…" He looked around, snapped a bag of potato chips off a clip rack and threw it on the counter. "Some chips."

Outside the store, Robin was just drunk enough to wobble on the steps and fall over. Clutching his bag close, he did not spill the goods. He was not drunk enough, though, to yield to his truest impulse and slug the liquor down right there. He carefully paced a hundred yards down the road, flung the bag of chips aside, tore the cap off the little bottle of whiskey and downed half of it in one burning draught.

In his mind he visualised a beast, coming fast upon the campsite, bearing ugliness and no discernible soul. Robin stumbled to the picnic table, climbed on top and lay belly down, head hanging over the edge, eyes boring into the blackness of the pup tent. No discernible soul.

Yup.

I'm your vulture, baby.

Your vulture.

He considered a move, saw it for what it was, knew he should think about it, knew he would not. He began the move, silently off the table, a sneak approach. He propelled with his arms, slinking sideways, onto the bench and onto cold ground. He crawled.

The tent flap was not secure and yielded at the nudge of his hand. There was no resistance. Inside the tent, his fingers sensed the downiness of hair, and the first of the warmth. Robin entered the tent, crawling.

For a long moment he was lulled by a beautiful heat, a thing he did not expect. A body-length oozing of joyous calming and comfort. The muscles of his shoulder and neck eased, lowering his profile. His fists unclenched. He tried to sense what was in the air, what it was that was taming him.

Welcome. A passionate and unearned acceptance. In his alcohol confusion, the mechanisms of his brain would not function. He proceeded and accepted with no understanding of why. He smelled her hair, then the musk released from her sleeping bag. In a rush, he was not tame any longer.

The sleeping bag yielded, like the tent flap, and the woman was revealed. With the remainder of his consciousness, Robin expected resistance, prepared to battle, but then...

A hand was there, touching. She took him into the bag as he searched her body with his tongue.

10

Toward morning, soul wakening, Robin tried to rise up and out in search of more liquor.

He thought of where his money was, somewhere in a buried pair of jeans in the mess of sleeping bag and tent. The need for drink was strong. As he struggled, a hand went to his neck, caressing. There was softness and care that did not stand consistent with what he was beginning to remember. Lulled, he began to fade. The dusky morning quieted him beyond the booze-lust, and the rumpled bed was warm and had features for him.

It is probably noon, Robin thought, maybe one or two o'clock, by the way the sun blazed into his closed eyes.

He knew he must turn his head before opening his eyes, or be blind for days.

His neck hurt. He rolled away from the glare, opened his eyes and saw that he was half in, half out of the tent, though most of him still occupied the sleeping bag. There was no sign of Norma.

Norma!

What happened?

What happened last night happened.

He remembered it. As bad as his drinking ever was, he always remembered. Then there would be the effort at forgetting.

But he couldn't do that this time. There was a witness. A victim.

Victim.

"Hi!"

The sound of her voice cut him. His head seemed split, pain from one ear to the other. His mouth was dry as pavement. He looked up, his pants half on.

"Good morning," she said. "Or afternoon."

She had been for groceries, held a bag full and wore a wide smile.

Robin stared, holding his shirt.

Norma set the bag down on the picnic table, fluffed her hair with both hands and stretched to the sky, as if she'd just got back from an aerobics class. Robin avoided looking at her, finished buttoning his shirt and zipping his jeans.

"Look," he said, standing straight amid the tangle of tent and sleeping bag, "I…"

"Have an orange." She tossed him one.

He caught it, not thinking, then there was a stinging in his hand. Did she throw it too hard? He held the orange.

She smirked. "We sure made a mess of that tent."

"Look." He tried but couldn't get the darkness off his face. "Look…"

"I bought the booze."

"What?"

"Next time, let's do it clean."

"Clean?"

"They say it's better with all your senses. I know it is."

"I didn't mean to. That wasn't me."

"No?"

"I don't do things like that."

Her smile faded. She looked at the ground. Robin felt something he had not expected. Her look was sadness, it penetrated to his bones. He wanted to cry.

She looked up, to his eyes. "I hope not," she said.

"How can I tell you how sorry I am?"

"Eat your orange," she said.

Then she shuffled through the grocery bag for some breakfast, casual. Robin, only a little relieved, knew it wasn't over.

They drove southwest on I-90. Sixty miles went by before Robin was comfortable enough to say: "How you doin'?"

Norma opened her eyes from a light sleep. The day was warm but hazy, almost grey in some places. High, thin cloud. Robin could see the wateriness of her eyes through her sunglasses.

Lack of sleep. His fault.

"Great."

Then silence.

The road went on. The VW ate the distance with a hearty dull rumble from its motorised bowels.

What did happen last night?

The notion of it, the idea that he might be a truly bad man, a woman abuser, Sex Offender, was so horrible he could barely acknowledge that it was he, Robin Wallenco, who was even thinking about it.

He tried to recall the exact events.

She had been there for him, it was obvious now, thinking about it. Open. In his state of mind, in his booze-haze, he hadn't questioned it, this openness. The warmth inside the sleeping bag.

Robin went over it in his head. All the movements. He'd never known a girl like this. So open.

He kept thinking about it. All about it. He forgot his fear, any revulsion he might have experienced when considering the moral aspects, the legal and ethical and common decency questions about the thing. His memory caressed the evening. Every move. He was getting hard, like a teenager.

He struggled to drive carefully.

He was startled when Norma said: "I love to fuck, you know."

"What?"

"You heard me." She laughed, a short harsh sound.

"Kind of unusual to hear. Just out of the blue."

"I'm always ready. I don't often meet people I like enough, but I'm always prepared. I'm on the pill, carry condoms, the whole bit."

"Very nice."

"Want to know how you rate?"

"Come on…"

"I've got this rating system. You get points off for being drunk."

"This is stupid."

"No it's not."

"Can't we talk nice?"

"Nice?"

"Yeah."

"What's nice about being raped?"

"I thought you liked…"

"To fuck. Or make love, if I like the guy. But you get points off for drunken rape. That's the rules."

"You said it was okay."

"On a scale of one to ten, with points off."

"Aw, for crying out loud…"

"What's the matter?"

"This is nuts. You're crazy."

"Crazy?"

"So am I, for getting involved with a fucking kid."

"A fucking kid. *Fucking* kid!"

"Shut up."

"You want to let me off?"

"Funny you should mention."

"Go ahead."

"I will."

"Go ahead."

"Where's the map? Where's the next rest stop?"

"It won't say. Just leave me here."

"I can't do that."

"Why?"

"It's the middle of nowhere."

"That's where you picked me up."

They rode ten miles to the next rest stop. As they pulled in and motored past the semi-trailer parking area, toward the rest rooms and a stand where local Lions Club members wearing bright blazers were handing out free coffee, Robin heard what he thought was a sob.

When she got out, he tried to see her face, but failed amid the hair-flinging fury of her rising from the car, wrenching the packsack out and stomping away without closing the door.

Robin watched her go. She strode strong, without looking back. Then he turned away, slammed his door, went around the car and slammed hers.

He wandered to the rest rooms with his hands in his pockets and arrived at a urinal without a conscious decision to pee. He unzipped. There were other travellers standing about, pissing, combing their hair, drying their hands at obnoxiously loud hot air dryers.

Something in the artificial heat of the place, the noise, and the way one half-bald fellow kept on combing a place on his scalp where there was no hair, it all came at him in anger. Inexplicable, he knew, irrational, forceful and dangerous. He was shocked at how merciless his emotion was, what it was forcing him to feel. He was glad he wasn't behind the wheel at that moment.

The dryers shrilled. Robin hastily zipped, the cloth of his jeans catching in the metal teeth. He struggled, cursing.

Unbearable.

Robin ran out of the place.

He stumbled, caught himself, walked fast, away from the rest rooms, into the middle of a grassy island of smoking truckers and families with frisbee-throwing kids. It was good to move his body, work it off.

He approached the coffee stand. A beaming Lion, rotund and happy, poured coffee into a Styrofoam cup.

"You look like you need a little pause, friend."

Robin took the cup absently.

"Watch it. Hot."

"Yeah, thanks."

Robin worked his way toward the car, holding the

cup, thinking. Then he was at the VW with no place left to walk.

Go. She can't be far.

Thinking hard, trying to figure out what to say, he took a hearty gulp of coffee.

"AAAH...!"

He dropped the cup. It hit the pavement and coffee splashed his shoes. His fingers were burning, his mouth nearly anaesthetised by the scalding heat. People nearby turned their attention to him. Robin swore, got into the car, started up and roared off to the exit.

Norma was standing a hundred yards from the rest stop, her head bowed, without her thumb out. The sight of her made his heart want out of his chest; the thought of her distress was poison to him. He slowed the car, wondering if he would be able to speak with a burned tongue.

She started walking when she saw him. He leaned over, rolled down the window. She did not look at him.

"What's the matter with you, anyway?" He had to yell above the traffic roar.

"Ask yourself."

"I asked you first."

"You'd never understand."

"Gimme a chance."

"Forget it."

Pause. She walked. He slowly drove.

"You'd be surprised," he called.

She walked.

"I think I see something in you. I think I know I see. There's something familiar about you. I can't quite get what it is, but..."

"Forget it."

"No."

Maybe she was melting a little. But she kept on walking.

"This is hard for me to say…"

"Why?" She stopped, facing him.

He stopped too, a lull in the traffic easing the noise a little.

"A couple of things," he said. "One, it might not be such a good thing, what I see. It's familiar, but I don't know if it makes me feel right, you know?"

"Well thank you. What's the other thing?"

"I burned my mouth with coffee. My tongue's got blisters on it."

She walked again, determined, ignoring him as he drove beside her. He did not see a smile develop, but knew that when she laughed things would be better.

She began laughing heartily, still moving forward. Then the laugh got so intense she had to stop walking. Robin chuckled, even with the pain in his mouth. He pulled over.

She guffawed, openly, holding her stomach. Tears began to form. She looked at him, hilarious, and laughed harder.

Two semi-trailers passed close beside them on the highway. Robin, through his chuckles, watched her laugh amid the roaring wind and noise.

She stopped laughing.

They looked silently at each other, the traffic blaring. Her eyes were hard, but Robin saw a hint of a grin was left on her lips. He wasn't sure whether it might be a good thing or a bad thing.

11

They took a motel room to clean up, to speak in civilised surroundings, and to decompress over dinner. She told him she had not fully understood herself, but that she had made love to him freely. Had planned it, even.

"You did?" he said.

"Of course. Couldn't you tell?"

"Well you didn't say anything."

"Neither did you."

They accepted that things had gone awry and easily, playfully resolved to keep things clear to each other in future. They spoke of many things, laughed a lot. They made love in their motel bed that night and Robin did not care if he woke up dead, because he was away from his cares and worries, floating on this unexpected cloud. They set off the next morning after a communal shower, he growing hard as she soaped his back, impromptu sex in the falling water.

Camping in the Bighorn Mountains of north-central Wyoming, they shared coffee and food by a campfire. The not-too-far-off howl of a coyote salted the session with old west movie-set authenticity.

Robin shuddered at the sound. "Jeez, could be real wild out here. Wish I'd brought a shotgun like a real man."

"Don't be silly. They never bother humans. And I wouldn't be with you if there was a shotgun along."

"If you weren't along that would be real scary."

"I'm sure you'd manage. Even without a gun."

"Don't like 'em, eh?"

"Nope."

"Well, neither do I, I guess…"

"You wouldn't need to guess if you'd seen what I've seen."

"What, you mean growing up in cowboy gun-action central? Home of the NRA, the KKK, and the anti-NAACP?"

"Yes to all but not even that. I lost the only boyfriend I ever had because of a gun."

"Oops."

"Don't worry, I'm over it."

"Holy shit."

"I shouldn't be talking like this. It's not that wild a story. I'm glad I'm not drinking."

"Why?"

"Because I might tell it to you."

"I think you should anyway."

"No I shouldn't."

"Why?"

"It'll change things."

"Things are always changing."

"Boy, you can sure fluff-talk when you want to."

"That's a cute way of putting it. But you're still gonna have to tell me."

"I don't have to do anything. That's why I travel."

"Sorry. But my interest is piqued."

"I've noticed something about you."

"What? But don't try to change the subject."

"What's this thing about violence with you?"

"You noticed."

"It's kind of hidden, but you've had your hands on me a few times now and, enjoyable as it's been, there's something scary there."

"Let me know if I'm too much."

"Of course, and I don't think you're into hurting. I'm kind of an expert on the subject. But there's a violence in the way you make love. Other women must have told you."

"Probably. Not in so many words. Not honestly."

"I'll let you know if I don't like it."

They leaned together for a kiss. Robin touched her hair, conscious of being extra gentle.

"This is all very fine," he said. "But you've changed the subject."

"That's what I get for being with a bright guy. Mostly I just get to talk to truck drivers and salesmen. They don't do this to me."

"What kind of stuff do they do?"

Norma stiffened and pulled away slightly. In the firelight he could see that his words and her thoughts were changing things between them. An immediate fear crossed his heart. "Maybe we better not talk anymore right now," he said.

She ran a hand through her hair, sighed and looked into the flames. Robin tossed a piece of wood into the embers, hoping the physical action might untie this unexpected emotional stalling. The silence of it was discomfiting.

"Actually, I think it might be a good idea," she said after a moment.

"Only if you think it is."

"I'm not sure how I feel with you. Safe, a bit, but there's something else. You're weird, Robin, that's all I can say."

"Thanks, I think."

"No, really. If I tell you this, no kidding, I'll just die if you change the way you look at me."

"Uh oh…"

"Should I stop?'

"Of course not. You can't now, can you?"

"No."

"Okay, then. Cast it to the wind. What's so terrible?"

"I could be doing jail time. I could be getting it up the ass with a broom handle from some ugly dyke-hag in maximum security or wherever. I could be buried in the ground with holes in my face. Nobody knows this story, at least not the whole thing. That's how I lost Bobby. You've got to tell me now that you'll never tell anybody else about this. Not even somebody far off in the future after you haven't seen me for a lifetime. Never. You can't tell anybody, not even me, because I never want it told to me again. Ever. I hate the fucking thing and I hate the fucking world when I think of it. It's like I could burn through the ground when I think of it, I'm so crazy…"

"Tell it, quickly."

"When I was in high school…I finished high school by the way; what I told you was bullshit."

"Whatever."

"I'm not seventeen. I'm almost twenty-two. I don't

know why I tell people I'm younger. Maybe that's just the way I feel…"

"Whatever. Please tell the story before we have the China Syndrome on our hands."

"Okay, Bobby was my boyfriend when I was in tenth grade. He was two ahead of me, so the next year I used to hitchhike over and visit him at UC, Sacramento. He was doing an agricultural science program. He wanted to become a super-farmer and I wanted to be his super-wife. I loved him; he was the only boy I ever had any interest in all through school. I know you wouldn't believe it to know me now but, I mean, he and I were sacred; it was the only good thing in my life. We didn't even have sex, for goodness sake. We were saving it. I knew we would be happy. It was all perfect and we had these great weekends with each other in California. I couldn't wait to finish school and move there. I was even thinking about dropping out just so I could be with him.

"One Thursday night I left school in the afternoon and started thumbing west. I'd always got good rides because I'm a girl and I'd always got the public service announcement speech from my mom and my teachers about not hitchhiking but nothing could stop me. It was visiting Bobby that got me used to it. It was scary at first, but I got the hang of it and it was the only way I could afford to see him. I got a good ride right through Nevada all the way to the other side of Las Vegas. Then a trucker took me to the California border. It was early in the morning, and I ate at this little place somewhere in the mountains. Diners were always good places to pick up rides because you could pick your personality, check out the driver and find out if they were going your way. Anyway, I started talking to this guy who said he was a student, too. He was about your age and looked pretty clean.

"He said he was going all the way to San Francisco, so it was looking really good. We went a little way and then, what I should have twigged on right away, not that it would have made any difference, but what should have set off the warning signs was that he didn't know the way to where he said he was going. I had to tell him what exit to take and then what Interstate to get onto and all the rest of the stuff. I guess I was so intent on getting to Bobby that I just ignored all the stuff I take good care about now. But then things seemed okay and we drove all morning into California and got close to Sacramento and this guy started getting weird, talking funny and eventually it got on to sex and he came right out and said he wanted to fuck me, in those words.

"I still didn't think things were out of control and thought he was just doing a clumsy job of coming on to me. I tried to be polite about it and let him down easy but then he reached under his seat and out came this ugly fucking gun, pointed at my head. He swerved a little and almost lost it, pointing the thing right at me. He had the front of the thing right on my cheekbone and started screaming like a nutcase about how he wasn't going to get ripped off by fucking bitches any longer and blah blah blah about his last girlfriend and how she'd made his life miserable and etcetera about all the usual misogynistic crap guys get on to when they're on a roll like that.

"I never had anybody point a gun at me before. After about a half-hour I noticed I was wet all over. I'd pissed my pants. He smelled it and calmed down, almost got apologetic, but he switched hands with the gun, steering and aiming with his left, and put his other hand into my jeans.

He reached all the way down, through my panties and stuck a finger up me. He started losing control of the car and pulled his finger out and started rubbing his hand over his face, smiling and saying things like he loved me and why don't we do this nice and whatever. He stopped the car at an auto court on a small highway just out of Sacramento and parked close to the office door. He held the gun low and looked me in the eyes and said he'd have the thing pointed at me through his jacket all the time he was out of the car. If I moved I was dead. He went in and got a room and drove us to a cabin out back.

"When we got into the place he told me to take off all my clothes but not to shower because he liked the smell of piss on me. Then he got on the bed and took his dick out of his pants and started to play with it, gun in one hand, limp dick in the other. He couldn't get a hard-on, so he eventually had me rubbing it, pulling it, sucking it, everything to try to get it hard. All the time he just lay back on the bed, gun pointed at my head. I mean, he had me in his clutches, he didn't need to have me covered all the time like that. I was naked, I couldn't just run, the door was locked, he had his clothes on and all that. It was weird but it was typical, you know? I've heard of similar situations so often it's almost commonplace. I was even thinking that while he was doing this to me, trying to make it less bad in my mind.

"After a while he started to get mad about his lack of erection. I mean, I did everything he told me to do, even tried to force it up me and sucked on it 'til I was dry and all the disgusting things you can think of, but then he hit me with his hand then belted me with the barrel of the gun. I was determined not to cry. That made him mad, but his prick was getting a little bit hard so he roughed me up some

more, threw me on my back and forced my legs apart. Then
the thing that hurts me the most to think of and that I'm
not going to talk about happened. But I think you know
anyway what took place."

"I can guess."

"I'm sure you can."

"Should I say it and then we can get past it?"

"Okay."

"He raped you with the gun."

"I wouldn't even call it rape so much, believe it or not.
He was gentle, inserted the barrel so slowly I almost
thought it was him but then I struggled and I knew it was
metal. He worked it up as far as it would go. It was hurting
but it could have hurt more if he'd moved it around or
something like I expected him to but he just moved it all
the way up and left it there for the longest time until I started getting totally sick about what he was up to. I guessed
he had his finger on the trigger. I couldn't see him, lying
back, but he was down there with his face in my crotch
thinking up something sick to do because his cock would-
n't inflate. I got beyond scared and went all cold, thinking
about the way I would be when he pulled the trigger. That
cold I still have inside me. I feel it whenever I know it's time
to move and get away. It's there whenever I want it to be and
sometimes when I don't. He just stayed there and then he
flopped over, crying, with his limp dick in his hand. I guess
he'd been trying to jerk off and it wouldn't work.

"He rolled onto his stomach and cried away like a
baby, whining about his mother and other sick things.
When I realized he'd went away from my crotch I reached
down and carefully got the gun out of me. It was the first
time I'd held a handgun. We had rifles and things at home

but I never had much to do with them. I just stared at it for a minute, then sat up and tried to think of what I could do to get out of there and get back to my life and see Bobby. It was the only thing I wanted to do. The guy was crying away into the bedspread and I sat there, not knowing what to do, with the cold still in me, shivering cold even though it was warm in the room. I could only think of Bobby. But I couldn't move. I was afraid and I guess I was just waiting for the guy to tell me to do more bad stuff and I couldn't move off that bed for anything. I felt like I was glued there.

"The shivering got so bad I guess he sensed it and rolled over to look at me and started laughing. He looked at me holding the gun and laughed, pointing. I looked at myself. I'd forgotten I was naked, with bruises all over me and the smell and pain was in me, all the way in me. Sitting there, aching, I just pointed the gun at him and pulled the trigger. He shouted just then so I didn't know if it had gone off or not. The barrel was thin, so I guess it wasn't a very powerful gun. The only thing that I remembered later was that there was smoke between us, the fumes of the powder going off, and he pointed at me shouting. Then he was crying again and blood was on his shirt. I pulled the trigger again and he rolled off the bed and started walking to the door. I ran after him and put the gun against his backbone and pulled the trigger again. He dropped like a rock right at my feet, crying like a sick calf and struggling with his arms. I wanted him to stop making noise. I put the gun against his chest and shot him again. There was hardly any sound. The bullet and the smoke and the noise I guess all just went into the hole I made in him and he stopped crying, stopped moving. He stared at me a long time without blinking and I realized he was dead.

"I went back and sat on the bed and had a good cry, holding the gun. I looked at it. There was blood on the front of it and specks on my hand. The barrel was glistening and then I knew that I'd killed somebody with a gun that had my vaginal fluid all up and down it and I felt like I might explode right there and then like a firecracker, and splash myself all over the walls and be unrecognisable to everybody in the world. I thought of Bobby, not knowing what to do. Then I got up, washed, and put on my clothes. I walked out the door and to the road and then walked around for awhile. It was evening; people were sitting in their houses, having dinner. I didn't know what to do but it was good to walk, fresh air on my face. It started to get dark. I got the shakes again, shivering bad, and realized I had to do something fast or I'd end up in the hospital with exposure or in shock or something. I came to a phone booth. I dialled the number of the university residence and got Bobby on the phone. I couldn't speak much, but begged him to come over and get me right away.

"It was about an hour's drive but he made it in forty-five minutes. He picked me up on the street and tried to get me to tell him what happened. I couldn't bring myself to and just told him to drive out of town and away from the place. We were almost past the motel when I realized I had to get my stuff from the guy's car. I told Bobby to park on the street and I'd be back in a minute. My plan was to sneak back into the room, get the keys, get my stuff and take off. In the room I had to look for a minute to find the keys. The guy was where I'd left him. Nobody seemed to be around. I got the keys and then Bobby was at the door, looking at me with eyes I'd never seen before and gasping and almost fainting. I ran to him but he bolted out the door and back to the car, swearing, gagging, carrying on. I don't know what freaked me more, the idea of killing somebody or having Bobby come apart on me like that.

"We peeled out of there and onto the Interstate. Bobby didn't say a thing to me all the way except that I stank like piss. Then he stopped at a rest area and opened his door and threw up on the pavement. I felt so sorry. I started apologising and pleading with him to be okay. He wouldn't say anything but went all quiet and cold with me. We drove to Sacramento and through town. I wanted him to take me to his room but he wouldn't even talk to me. Then he stopped outside the bus station, dug in his pocket and gave me a couple of twenty-dollar bills.

"I pleaded with him again. He just looked at me with dead eyes and said, Norma, I want you to go home now and never come here again. No Bobby, I said, we can be okay; I'll go to the police and tell them the truth and everything will be okay. But he just leaned over me and opened the door on my side and said Norma I want to be a doctor. I've been accepted at veterinarian's college and if I want to get licensed I can't afford to have anything to do with this. Even if you didn't murder the guy, we've both committed a crime by running away. Things are only going to get worse. Don't tell a soul about it. Never say a thing about it. If you do, I'll come after you. So help me christ I'll tell them you're the worst slut of a road-hounding hose bag I've ever met. I should have known something like this would happen. I never want another thing to do with you. Now go away.

"He reached into the glove compartment and pulled out a shiny little gun and showed it to me. Then he said, if you ever come near me again, I'll shoot you in self-defence, understand?

"I couldn't move. The sight of another gun did it to me. Bobby pushed me out on the street, threw my bag after me and took off. I never saw him again."

Norma moved her feet a little away from the fire. She shifted her position on the bench beside Robin.

"I didn't take the bus. I started hitchhiking in any direction I could get a ride. I didn't go home for months. When I did, I just finished school and left again the day after graduation. The rest you know. It isn't important…" She paused, ruffled her hair and sighed. "It's the one thing I'll tell you," she said.

"I…" Robin could not say anything further.

"Nobody knows."

"Of course."

Later, after a cup of tea, Robin said: "I guess the saddest part is Bobby and you."

"Are you kidding? Bobby and me. It never would have worked, now that I look back on it. He was too clean."

"Hmmm. Well, I think on balance he was a little dirty, but that's neither here nor there. I guess you might be right. Still, even though it was years ago, you still must suffer from it."

"I can't cry."

"I can."

"You're lucky."

"Think so? It comes at awkward times. Times that show me I'm not dealing with anything, always running away. I know this and see the signs but still I never change. I've done things I cry about, but I never change."

"Like what?"

"Like listening to your story. It makes me want to cry."

"Don't bother. It won't help. What other things make you cry?"

"Oh god, do I have to go into it...?"

12

"I guess it's my turn," Robin said as they sped onto the morning-quiet Interstate entrance ramp and away from their story-telling camp. He squinted into the brilliant dry-land sun glancing in from the east, cutting his eyesight to the left and making the interior of the car a series of near-horizontal illustrated sections.

Norma glanced at him under a raised hand to shade her eyes. "I let you off last night because we were tired and the mood was heavy."

"No kidding. A blow-out saga like that. You could write a book."

"Never. For you only. Promise you'll never tell."

"I promise, I promise. What's the big deal, anyway?"

"I have nightmares sometimes, thinking about if they ever arrest me."

"Yeah, I guess there's that."

"I never go to California."

"Good idea."

"Never."

"You covered your tracks pretty well by the sound of it."

"Yes, but you never know."

They drove in ruminative silence, the side-lit landscape rushing by dramatically.

"So," Norma said, "do you have a turning-point saga to sling to me, or are you going to let me just use my imagination?"

"Turning point? I'm not sure."

"Well whatever."

"I guess I could tell one."

"Only if you want to."

"I suppose."

"This is tiring."

"I'll try to make it short."

"Don't worry, I'll stay awake."

"It's nowhere near as awful as yours."

"That's nice."

"I feel like a fool even mentioning it. It's so minor."

"Tell it!" She swayed with emphasis, nudging him gently sideways. The car swayed in its lane as he corrected. "It'll make me forget mine."

"You have to promise not to grab the wheel at any point."

"Maybe I should drive, so you can concentrate."

"That won't be necessary."

"It will if I kill you for keeping me in suspense all the time."

"Gotcha. In that case let me tell you about my life back in the city when I was getting un-married. As a way to avoid drinking I'd go to movies. You couldn't find me half the time. I went to a lot more movies than the average person. The only person who maybe went to more was a guy I came to call The Groaner. I mean, he turned up at the ones I went to all the time so you've got to figure that, unless there was some kind of monster coincidence going on, he must have gone to all those movies lots of times over.

"I wish like hell he hadn't. The Groaner was a head case; old clothes, dirty face. Never shaved. Always sat in front where I like to be and groaned at the racy parts. The only time I got a break was when there were pretty girls around. He liked to give them creepy looks before the show. Then when it was dark and there was a sexy part he groaned and made other sounds, moving around in his seat as if he was letting a giant fart. The girls usually left at that point. These weren't crummy places I'm talking about. These were the places decent people go to watch movies. They had to put up with this kind of stuff.

"So people said I was avoiding things by going to so many movies. They were right, I guess. Mostly I avoided people who said I was avoiding things all the time. I had lots to avoid, let's face it. My place was a bit of a dump, I admit. I hated the joint but it was all I could afford with my expenses. I was going to school in those days and paid the bills with this part-time job as a draughtsman. Hated the job, but it was the kind of place where, if you did your work fast, you could goof off for the rest of the day, usually enough time to hit a matinee or two.

"I had a soon-to-be ex–wife I was trying to forget. We had tried it a couple of times by then and I think we tried again a few more times after that, but at that point Sheila was getting on my nerves. She wanted to talk about why I was late with my cheques or why I didn't see my folks who she's still close with. I just tried to change the subject or hang up the phone. She'd get off lines like: You're just a dreamer, and: You're never going to be happy, etcetera. Her theory was that I was escaping by going to so many movies.

"And she was right. One day I was working very hard to finish a contract so I'd be able to catch a mid-afternoon show downtown. I worked at it like crazy. My supervisor had complained about smudges—this was in the days before computers—so it took more time than usual and I didn't make the afternoon show. I got to the first evening show and who should be there but the goddamn Groaner. As usual the bastard sat right beside me and as usual he had the buzzard breath which floated over once in a while and made me think I was going to puke. I just couldn't take him that day for some reason and I thought about moving farther up so I couldn't smell him. But why should I move when he was the problem?

"So I said hey, you. How about moving off to the side, eh? You smell. A couple of people looked when I said that and I was embarrassed. But somebody had to do something. The Groaner just leered over at me and didn't say anything, didn't even look like he'd understood I was talking to him. Lucky for me, a couple of minutes later some girls came in and sat at the end of our aisle. He went and sat by them.

"After the show I was hungry and went for eats. And after that I didn't know what to do and checked the paper for something I hadn't seen. There was some teen flick playing and I couldn't remember if I'd seen it or not because it had a number on it. *CHEM LAB PART FIVE: THE REVENGE.* I know I'd seen part three, the one about the beach party and I'd seen another one too but I couldn't remember if it had been the fourth or fifth. I checked my pocket for money. Five dollars. Three short. I booted over to a bank machine. Taking out the minimum ten dollars left me two bucks short on Sheila's support cheque.

"I found a booth and phoned and told her the situation. She flung me the usual abuse, topping it with: My God, I don't know why I'm surprised. Anyone can see you're helpless. Hopeless. Next thing I know you'll be losing your job, if you haven't already…Have you been drinking?

"I hung up on her. I was almost late for the show, I had to hurry. I was never so happy to see an empty theatre. Usually these weekday features were good for that. A couple of teenagers came in as the lights were going down, but they sat way in back. I was just trying to decide if I'd seen it or not when sure as shit, the lumpy, ugly stinking Groaner scudded down the aisle and came over and sat right in front of me. An empty theatre and the stinking skunk sits right in front of me."

Robin stopped to allow Norma to finish her giggle.

"Great, you're laughing."

"Maybe not laughing, chuckling."

"Whatever. Considering what you've been through, anything short of a primal scream would be success."

"You might have a future in stand-up."

"I hope you won't mind if I remain seated."

"Quit being silly and get on with it."

"Thank you. Anyway, The Groaner settled in his seat and let out a good one, a long low moan, as one of the girls on the screen took off her jogging shorts in a locker-room scene. I could see I was in for it. I tried to concentrate. The movie was about this group of kids with this mean-but-kind-of-nice-looking chemistry teacher who makes them do lots of extra studying. To get back at her they break into the school at night and have a party in the lab, doing all kinds of weird experiments.

"They made an explosion and blew the clothes off this one girl. The Groaner groaned. They covered each other with KY jelly and slithered around on each other. The Groaner did a series. One of the girls smeared herself with dye and stamped an outline of her ass on the teacher's desk. The Groner horked a few times and let out a savage fart.

"Needless to say, I couldn't enjoy the movie. Every time I got into what was going on, The Groaner would out with one and bring me back. It was driving me crazy. Finally I just couldn't stand it any more and leaned forward and growled in the guy's ear as snarly as I could. He didn't move, didn't say a thing. One of the girls on the screen got splashed with water and you could see her nipples through her shirt. He yelped out loud. I leaned over again, stabbed my finger into his shoulder and snarled at him: Quiet, old man. He turned around slow. I could tell before I saw his face he'd have that grin going. He snickered, like a kid, and raised his loony eyebrows. He looked at me a long time. Then, surprise surprise, he got up and lurched away, down the row. Gone.

"By that time the picture was half over. The kids opened this supply room at the lab and let this ugly creature out that one of the kids discovers is actually the wicked chem teacher in her true form. Every kid but one gets ripped to ribbons and the last one only gets away by pouring acid on the thing and limping away before the whole school goes up in flames. Maybe you've seen it?"

"We weren't allowed to see movies like that."

"No? Hmm. I guess there's a pro and a con. It never did me any harm, don't you think?"

"Don't try to make me laugh anymore. Just go on with the story."

"As you wish. Anyway, I remembered that I actually had seen the movie before, but stayed while they rolled the credits because I wanted to see if they had made a CD of all the songs. By the time the credits were through and the lights were on, there wasn't anybody there but me and the usher, going through the rows with a garbage bag.

"In the lobby I could see it was pitch black outside because it was almost midnight. I needed to piss, and ducked into the men's room so I wouldn't have to look for a safe place on the walk home. I was standing at the urinal, halfway through, when the door opened and I heard that familiar shuffling sound. I didn't have to look to know who it was. The Groaner moved up to a urinal and made to open his fly. Then he looked at me, and I wondered how he'd got in; he hadn't been in the lobby when I was there. He plunged his hands down into his overcoat without undoing his fly and stepped toward me. I finished up and started to do up my zipper when a blast of his breath nearly knocked me over. I turned to him, still fiddling with my pants. He grabbed my throat, bear-gripped like steel, and rammed a fist into my gut.

"I'd barely zipped. That was my thought, hanging by The Groaner's grip, not the pain or the blueness of my eyesight. He lifted me off the floor and threw me across the room. I splatted on the cold tile and slumped. With both hands he grabbed me by the coat and dragged me back to the sinks. He held me up to the mirror, shook me a couple of times, made weird sounds.

"We stood there. The Groaner looked at me in the mirror with flamed-out pupils and once in a while shook me like a half-dead rabbit. Then he threw me across the room again and I passed out. There was no light when I woke up. All there were were colours, shades of blue against the black. Some red. There was a hell of a pain everywhere, as if somebody had attached a giant rubber band around my forehead.

"I gradually got my arms working. After a while I picked myself up and felt the way to the door. I stumbled out to the lobby. It was dark except for the exit signs over the doors. I realized: I'd been rolled by The Groaner! I felt for my wallet. It was still there. I stood for a while in the dead lobby, the smell of people everywhere. The doors to outside were right there; just a twist of a lock and I could leave this weird experience behind me. But I didn't care.

"I went for the seats, stumbled right away for my favourite spot, five rows from the front, smack in the middle. Sprawled across the armrests, holding my aching gut in the dark and quiet, I knew I could stay there my whole life."

Snickering passed, Norma's face had become serious again. "I love it," she said.

"I'm glad. Do you think it's true?"

She looked at him. He could see the basics of a smile in his sidelong glance, but that was all there was. Then he took another look and saw that her eyes were hard, holding tears that would not fall.

"It's where you belonged, right?"

"Yes."

"It's true," she said. "It's all true."

13

They stopped for gas outside Cheyenne, Wyoming. Robin, sweating in the dry heat, filled the tank and checked the oil. Norma went in search of coffee and something to munch on. She was good at scrounging. She would have to be, there were few buildings around this sparse, dusty place. Robin was closing the engine hatch as she returned, cups and bag in hand.

"Good man," he said.

"Woman."

"Whatever. Those doughnuts better be fresh."

"Muffins. Week old. This isn't the big city, you know."

Robin paid for the gas and joined Norma in the car.

"Something I've been meaning to tell you," he said. "I've got no money."

"Oh? What does that mean, exactly."

"It means, I got the gas. Here's the only serious cash, maybe a hundred and thirty dollars in bills. And I have, oh, about seventy cents left in my jeans. Here." He handed her coins.

"I like what else is in your jeans."

"Charming girl. But what do we do about the immediate problem? I had a fantasy about pulling some kind of bank card trick but…"

"Never mind. I've got money. Let's just get out of this place…"

Robin pulled the car away from the service station.

"Stop at that phone booth," she said.

"Okay. What's the matter?"

"Nothing. I want to phone."

The booth was dusty and crumbling.

Norma got out of the car, wordless. This was something different. In the three days they'd travelled together she hadn't spoken at all about family or friends, anyone she might like to call. She dialled the phone. Robin watched, expecting her to plunk the receiver down any minute because of a faulty phone, not serviced for generations, or because no one was home or there was a busy signal. After a short wait, she began to talk, sometimes animated, and Robin wished he had studied lip reading.

Wait a minute. Mind your own business.

Robin sat in the car, looking at the maps, trying not to watch her too closely.

In ten minutes she was back. Robin had actually been able to engross himself, plotting their course southeast. The tone of the car door closing, harsher than usual, alerted him. Norma smiled pleasantly but he could tell something was up.

"What?" he said.

"Nothing. I think I've got to go home for awhile."

"Oh?"

"No big thing."

"Well, no. Come on. Can I help?"

"You can drop me at a bus station when we get to Cheyenne."

"Whoa. That's a little abrupt, isn't it?"

"Why?"

"I've become accustomed to your face, to quote from somewhere."

Norma turned away. He stared out past the crumbling phone booth to wide prairie and craggy mesas a long way off where she seemed to be looking.

"You can't just turn away from me like that. I'm here. I'm not going away."

"No," she said. "I've got to think. Just drive."

Robin drove without being fully conscious of what he was doing. How could so much good spirit blow away in a few minutes on the phone? The outskirts of Cheyenne started before he had quite finished his coffee.

"I've got to call again," she said. "Find a phone."

He stopped at a McDonald's. The parking lot was full of big, brawny-looking cars and dusty trucks. Robin pulled the VW close to a telephone booth.

"Just wait," she said, getting out.

This time it was twenty minutes, and not so animated. He watched her face for clues. There were none. He found his questions turning into frustration and then anger. She slid back into the car. He had a country and western station wailing on the radio.

"It's my mother," she said. "I'm going home."

"You just want a lift to the bus station."

"Yes."

"Fuck you."

Norma did not react. Robin watched closely.

"Well?" he said.

"Well what?"

"What next?"

Norma turned to the back seat, grabbed her packsack and opened the door. Robin boiled.

"Get your fucking hands off that stuff and talk to me!"

He grabbed her wrist. She struggled. Through his heat, he had just enough perception to notice that this was a familiar thing to her. She shielded her face with a free hand.

"Don't…" she said.

He let her go. "I'm sorry."

She hurried out of the car. Robin got out and stomped around to her side as she extracted her stuff.

"Look, you can't just go like this. I feel like things aren't finished." He put a hand on her shoulder. She pulled away.

"This fella botherin' you, ma'am?"

A tall cowboy with the hat, the boots and the dust on his jeans, had come out of the restaurant, a half-eaten Big Mac in his hand. Norma looked at the cowboy, then Robin. She hoisted her load and began to walk toward the busy four-lane street. Robin stepped quickly after her.

"Can't we just talk?"

"This fella botherin' you, ma'am? Sure looks that way."

Robin looked at the cowboy. He wasn't much more than a kid, scrawny. He noticed a bundle of faces observing from inside the air-conditioned comfort of the restaurant. "It's okay, man. Private discussion."

"Ain't nobody call me man around here who drives one 'a these Kraut shithunks. Ain't no man to call anybody else a man."

"Look, pal, cowboy, John Wayne, whatever your name is. Butt out, eh."

The kid threw away the remains of his hamburger and walked with both hands away from his sides. Neither he nor Robin were quite keeping up with Norma. They reached the sidewalk.

"Norma, for crying out loud. Stop a second."

She had her thumb out to the traffic.

"Mister, you better have a good reason for botherin' this lady."

Robin faced the young man. "Look, I don't know any other way to say it. This is none of your business."

"That so, lady?"

Norma did not answer. A car slowed and pulled up.

"Now come on, wait a minute." Robin put his hand on her shoulder.

The cowboy gripped Robin's arm. Robin swung back, shrugging the arm away. The cowboy grabbed with the other arm, clinching Robin from behind and around the middle. Robin did not want to believe things were as out of control as he knew they were.

"Lay off!"

"Like hell, mister."

Robin twisted, got his footing, and pushed himself and the cowboy into the neatly maintained shrubbery. The cowboy whooped. A crowd gathered in the parking lot. Robin had so much dust in his eyes he couldn't see what was going on, but surprised himself with his sense of the struggle. He'd landed on top and taking the advantage, gripped the cowboy around the neck and choked with all the power in his hands.

The cowboy thrashed and cursed, trying to get a leg up and roll Robin away, but it was useless. He tried punching, but couldn't get any purchase in the dirt and the shrubs. Robin began to beat the cowboy's head into the ground.

"Whoa there, fellas." An older, conciliatory voice. "Cops are comin'."

Robin had the upper hand, eased his grip on the other man's throat and knelt on his chest, ramming his head back into the soil, forming an egg-shaped impression in the ground.

"Stop it!" An authoritative voice.

Robin heard it, understood it, but knew he would never stop, not now, not on his own. It was to the death. He knew it; it frightened him, it sickened him, but he knew it. The tension release, the pleasure, the strength like dark magic going to his arms and hands. His grip on the boy's throat was a puzzling lifeline, a conduit to sanity. The clarity of thought amid violence, the fine control made him gasp. He was in love with it then, had never felt a sensation like it…

I don't want to kill him, but I know I'm going to. I know I'll be sorry afterward, but I'm killing him anyway. That's all there is to it. That's all…

"Cut it out, boys."

A grip like steel tongs clamped Robin's neck and lifted him away from the prone cowboy. Uncoupled, Robin saw the cowboy's terror and was immediately relieved, like cool water on his face, glad to relinquish the black comfort of dead certainty he had had in the heat of fighting. The grip set him down on his feet. A tall man, a Marlboro cigarette ad man, in a deputy sheriff's uniform, hat, tin star and all, stood beside him.

Robin's head was light; he thought he might pass out. His knees semi-buckled. He resisted an impulse to lean against the Marlboro sheriff.

"Whatta you boys fightin' about?"

The dirtied cowboy got up from the ground. He and Robin stood, snuffling, rubbing their faces, and looked at each other.

"I don't hear anybody sayin' anything."

"It was nothing," Robin managed.

"This guy was botherin' a lady," the cowboy said.

"What lady?"

The cowboy and Robin looked around. Norma was gone. Thick traffic hummed around them.

"Well, she was here a minute ago. Got a ride, I guess."

"Musta done." The deputy turned to the people standing around, many chewing on hamburgers, sucking on soft drink straws. "Anybody see what was goin' on?"

A collective wilting hit the crowd. Those with soft drinks drank. Those with food chewed. A few turned and strode away.

"Okay," said the deputy. "Come on over to the cruiser, boys."

Robin and the cowboy walked together. "You sure can fight, mister."

Robin turned away, surprised at himself, unaware of what to say.

Where am I?

He looked hard at the cowboy.

In Wyoming, and I'm lucky this hayseed didn't draw a Colt .45 and perforate my brain. This is America, people carry firepower here.

"Fight?" he finally spoke to the cowboy. "I hardly ever fought in my life. Not men, anyway."

"Well, you sure had me down."

"Sorry."

"You musta had your reasons."

"Somewhere, I suppose."

The deputy leaned into the front seat of the cruiser and took out a clipboard. "What are your names?"

They told him.

The cowboy was a local named Walter. The deputy asked if he had anything more to say.

"Oh, I dunno, he's kinda okay after all, I guess."

"If that's the way you feel, don't pick fights."

"I learned my lesson."

"That's good. I'm gonna let you go now."

Walter left the scene.

The deputy read what he'd taken of Robin's name. "You're from where?"

"British Columbia."

"Up north, huh?"

"Right."

"Funny way for a tourist to act."

"I guess so. Sorry."

"Well," the deputy opened the cruiser door and threw in his clipboard, "this may be the Wild West, but it ain't like you see in the movies. Watch yourself."

"Thanks, I will."

The lawman drove off. Robin went into the McDonald's, washed up, and returned to the VW. Inside, he stared straight ahead, buzzing. He had pain in his side, ribs and back.

He started the car and drove out of the parking lot.

Three blocks later the street narrowed to two lanes and the buildings got older. It narrowed even more and Robin was driving through Old Cheyenne, a movie set, real John Wayne country but with buses and cars. Robin did not pay attention; he was hurting from the fight and a distressing absence in the car.

He stopped behind a bus off-loading tourists. He wished he could be in a daze and not feel. He almost wished he was still fighting.

He sat in the heat, idling in the midst of bumper-to-bumper traffic.

The street began to open a little and the buildings got newer. Robin took the first opportunity to swerve into a free lane as the street became modern again. He sped carelessly; stores, people, signs, shot by: Senor McTaco, Al's Sunrise Sombrero Mexican Dinner House, another McDonald's, the Central Cheyenne Greyhound Depot...

The tires of the VW squealed so loudly Robin did not know for sure that it was actually him making all that noise.

He thought about what he might say to her, if he found her, if he said anything to her, if she would even talk to him.

He parked and ran in. The place was bigger than he expected, maybe three hundred people strolling around, waiting on benches, buying tickets for who-knows-where. He started at the end by the street and worked his way to the other, where large doors led to banks of buses, loading and unloading. As he passed the ticket counter, he quickly tried to see if a bus had left for Arizona in the last hour.

But then there she was, sitting close to the big bus-loading doors, perched on a bench, feet on packsack. There was space beside her. He sat.

She stared blankly ahead.

"This is getting familiar," he said.

"What?"

"My running after you. Driving like crazy. I even fought for you. Because of you, anyway."

She looked at him. "I'm sorry. But I find it's the best thing to do. Solves all sorts of problems."

"I don't want you to be sorry." No response. He looked around, then back to her. "What problems?"

"Are you sure you want to get involved with me? I mean, more than you are already?"

"What's so horrible?"

"I don't want to get into that right now." She turned away again, fretting. Gently, he settled an arm around her.

"I'm glad you found me," she said. " I was feeling lost. More than usual."

"You? Lost?"

"Don't be that way. I'm serious. You don't want to know me."

"Don't you be that way."

"Look," she turned to him. "I'm glad you're back."

"Good."

She disengaged his arm, sat back and looked closely at him.

"Did you really have a fight?" She patted his shoulders. Dust rose.

"Where do you think this grit came from, and these puncture wounds?" Robin lifted his shirt.

"Some toughie, huh?"

He grabbed her packsack, rising. 'Well, ma'am. A man's gotta do what a man's gotta do…"

"Barf."

The town, she told him, was called Ascension City.

"Sounds holy," he said, driving.

"You'll see."

"Good."

"But it's out of your way."

"What's my way?"

"I don't know. You haven't told me."

"Just as well."

"How do I know it's just as well? You haven't told me. It must be important."

"Maybe it is, I don't know. Anyway, what's the problem at home? You said something about your mother."

"It's hard to explain."

"No it isn't. You choose your words, and say them one after another. When you're finished, you stop."

"I could say the same thing to you."

"Yes, you could, but then you wouldn't be respecting your elders."

"You're funny."

"Glad you think so. I repeat, what's up at home?"

"I'm not sure I can do anything. I just want to go and see. Then we can leave, if you want. I'm not finished travelling."

"Okay. But you're making it harder than it has to be."

"Why?"

"I could share this with you."

"No you can't."

"That makes it hard. For you and for me."

"You don't have to come if you don't want to."

"Yes I do."

"Why?"

"Because I don't want to go where I'm going just yet.
I'm not ready. This is better."

"Where are you going?"

"I forget."

"No you don't."

"For now, I forget."

Norma stared at him for a moment, then looked out
at the wide, dry landscape. Robin noticed in a quick sideways glance how her hair played in the rushing air. She
turned back to him.

"What made you forget?"

"Guess."

"No."

"Too bad."

"Ach…" She gripped his neck and throttled him gently as he drove. "You could have been arrested back there."

"All for you…"

14

Sometime late in 1944, trucks rolled into the compound and lights were turned on, rousing everybody from sleep. It was probably early morning. Soldiers paced in the snow, officers stamped around, smoking and speaking in low voices among themselves. The work leaders were called to conference and an hour later you were in a truck with the others, heading west.

Numerous times you were forced to abandon the trucks and repair broken bridges in your path. There were airplane attacks and many dead left by the side of the road. The big retreat is documented; your route apparently came to an end somewhere in the western fringes of the Ukraine. You were a single truckload at this point. One morning the artillery blasts were closer than usual, but what was particularly disturbing was that they seemed to be coming from up ahead instead of fading behind.

On a stop in a village an army officer stepped up and requested volunteers for a work project a few kilometres away. He offered hot food. No one came forward. Everybody wanted to get home. The fighting sounds were not a deterrent. Some of them must have been quite near their homeland at that point. There was not a sound from the huddled ranks. The blasting sounds and some smaller, popping and crackling noises only a few miles away, curdled your blood, made your spine like rubber. You might have shuddered, holding a biscuit, trying to drink your daily ration of brackish tea. The officer noticed you.

"You there. Volunteer?"

The others did not look at you, did not look at the officer. They bent to their steaming tea, warming their noses. The officer walked up to you and looked directly into your eyes.

"Volunteer?"

The word rang in the coldness for a moment, then was erased by the roar of a close-hitting shell. The sound reverberated in the buildings of the square and hurt your eardrums. The men tensed. Your hands shook, spilling hot tea on your fingers. The officer stood statue-still, a smile coming to his face.

"We go there," he said, pointing back to the east, away from the roar.

"*Ja,*" you must have said, or maybe you just quietly went along.

Any misgivings you may have had melted away when the truck carrying you and a load of supplies wheeled out of the village, headed north-east, and the fighting sounds faded. A hundred and fifty kilometres later you were in a compound of small buildings, several barracks, a parked half-track. The largest building was in the distance, puffing grey smoke through a high brick stack. There were few people about, although the place seemed set up to handle hundreds. A railway spur swung from the trees and ended just outside the gate. As you got down from the truck, the last group of cattle cars pulled away from the raised loading platform.

You might have taken a day or so to figure out what we know now. The place was called Solinjberg, after the town nearby, and it was one of those spots where people entered as human beings and left as shovels-full of ash. It was a relatively smaller operation as death camps went, but it had bid farewell to something like eighty-five thousand victims in two-and-a-half years.

Your assignment was to supervise the last slave barracks, about ninety men, in dismantling the place. The Russian advance was in full stride by that time, with Americans coming from the other direction. They figured you had about three weeks to do the job. You were given a stall at the end of the barracks in which to sleep. After the shrivelled inmates had unloaded the supplies, the officer went away with the truck. Three soldiers were left in the camp, one of them a sergeant.

And you, slave foreman.

The inmates unloaded boxes, sacks of grain, barrels of kerosene and case after case of explosives. Work on the camp started next day.

You organised a crew to take down the wire and fence emplacements, assigning small gangs to dig up the concrete ballast. Work began on the rail spur, digging up the ties, hauling the rails into the woods. All the buildings, except the last barracks and the guardhouse, were burned. The ashes and debris were then dug into the ground by the sullen, weak prisoners. You were surprised they could even stand up, let alone wield a shovel. They were given an amazingly small amount of food.

You joined the soldiers in the guardhouse for meals. A slave dutifully served as cook and valet. You ate relatively well, even better than in the early days of the work camp. The bony ghosts labouring their lives away outside did not get in the way of your appetite. The sergeant, whose name was Quartzmann, remarked on it.

"Hungry, my friend? Eat well. You'll never eat as well as here."

You said nothing, but smiled, chewing.

"Like this work?"

You smiled again.

"Like this work? Eh?"

An answer was required. You swallowed.

"*Ja.*"

"*Gut.* You might survive." He laughed, nudging the others. "He might survive, eh?"

They all laughed. You continued to smile, chewing.

The work went on. You were impressed by the quiet compliance of your workforce. In the first day, two of them dropped dead at their tasks. The others wordlessly transported their comrades' remains to a large pit at the edge of the woods. The next day two more were dead. On the third day only one. The next killed none but the day after that saw four deposited. It became apparent to you that most of the food supplies that had arrived with you were certainly not meant for these unfortunate skeletons.

Quartzmann laughed garrulously at mealtimes, slapping you on the back with exaggerated affection.

"Good job, foreman. Think you will finish? Eh? Your workforce going to last?"

The only work the soldiers seemed to have was the nightly cremation of dead slaves. You watched the glow of the kerosene fire flicker on the wall above your bunk.

When the last of the fencing was gone, the whole force got working on the foundations of the large building with the smokestacks. By now you knew what the furnaces inside were for, but to you it must have seemed like some ghastly experiment gone wrong, an isolated anomaly in a war that was a sea of anomalies. You were a walking anomaly all by yourself.

One of the soldiers was a sapper. He drilled charges into the concrete of the furnace building and blew the chunks into manageable pieces. Manageable by ordinary workmen that is. Your slim labourers had to gang up four on a rope to budge the pieces, drag them out of the camp locale and a few feet into the bush. You lost fifteen in three days of this activity.

But finally it was done and all that remained was the barracks you were living in and the guard hut. You were down to about forty-five workers by that time. Sergeant Quartzmann instructed you to have a good-sized trench dug out by the cremation hole before torching the barracks. You knew who that was for, but by now you must have wondered just what the plans were for you. You couldn't help thinking that maybe some little spot in this dark hole might be your final rotting place.

The slaves took two-and-a-half days to do the job. On the morning of the third day, the soldiers set fire to the barracks as the slaves worked. You saw in their faces that they knew this would be their last day. They'd seen dawn for the last time. Even though the weather was cloudy, threatening rain, they must have each found a new beauty in the simple act of drawing a breath.

Around noon the soldiers came out to the pit. They were jovial, swaying. You realised they were drunk. You were surprised and envious, having not seen any liquor in the supplies. They carried machine pistols instead of the usual rifles.

Quartzmann arranged it so that the slaves would not have much to think about. Sternly, he sent three of them back to stand by the guard house. He turned to you.

"Go with them. Make them stay."

The clicking of the machine pistols being cocked sounded loud as you walked away. By the time you got to the guard house Quartzmann had ordered the slaves into the pit. You didn't watch; three machine pistols chewing point blank at forty starved waifs only took about seven seconds. Once the shooting began, the forced joviality of the shooters faded, their mouths set in grim lines, their eyes reddened, unblinking. There were no cries from the victims. You couldn't look the three temporary survivors in the face.

Quartzmann approached, swinging his gun like a baton.

"Go," he said to the gaunt-eyed trio. "Cover."

They returned to the pit and watched as the last of the kerosene was spread, lit, and burned down. Lime was spread. Under the sapper's direction, they began digging holes along the sides of the pit. Quartzmann took your arm.

"Come, my friend. We eat."

They seemed to have kept the best food for last. The supplies were nearly gone but there were canned beans and biscuits with tea — even sausage — better food than you'd

had in years. You ate, uneasiness about the killings beginning to fade. Many people were dying, it's true, and I guess
you had to get used to it. In the close confines of the guardhouse, Quartzmann's breath was strong with alcohol. You
looked around for the bottle, but couldn't see it.

The meal was leisurely with the approaching end of
the work. What was next you did not know. A pounding
uneasiness gnawed at you. The smell of liquor was driving
you crazy—to forget this, to drift away even for a few hours
on a holiday of alcohol. What heaven! You feared you were
close to fainting. The other soldier came in to eat and
switched places with his comrade. These two were visibly
tanked, their jocularity forced but buoyed nonetheless by
blessed drunkenness.

Quartzmann poured you more tea.

You were developing, through the fear and the booze-
lust, an odd sense of this man. He was big without being
portly. His movements studied and intense. He seemed to
have an inner power and exercised a charismatic control,
more than just in the sense of his position as provisional
commandant of this doomed camp. The way he poured the
tea, with a strong wrist, eyes not on the cup but on you. I've
seen this man myself. He has a creepy way about him. And
here he was doing something to you and you didn't know
what it was.

You wished like hell you could have a drink. It had
been an unbelievable three years since you'd had anything,
even wine. You were going crazy thinking about it. You did-
n't want Quartzmann to see you like this. You downed the
tea in one slug, got up and went outside.

The last three slaves stood a distance from the pit,
their work at an end. The sapper laid charges in the holes.

Sergeant Quartzmann appeared, holding a large semi-automatic pistol. He motioned with the gun for the three shadows to go toward the guardhouse. He turned to you.

"Come, my friend."

When you were far enough away, the sapper tripped the switch on his hot-box and a series of small explosions collapsed the sides of the trench, burying all. It was a neat job; given the look of the terrain, the type of vegetation, you could see that eventually grass and weeds would take hold. A year from now, no one would immediately suspect what lay below. Then a light snow began to fall, and you were impressed by the notion that the horror would be hidden by suppertime.

At the guardhouse, Quartzmann led the three slaves inside and had them sit on a bench along one wall. He called for you to come in.

After the things you'd seen, almost nothing would have surprised you. Almost every possibility you could think of filled you with dread. He motioned for you to close the door. You noticed boxes of explosives set under the eating table, and wires leading out a window. The three shrunken men sat with their heads bowed. Quartzmann handed you the gun.

"You must be with us."

"I am with you."

"Not yet."

Outside, the two soldiers had thrown what little gear there was into the half-track. The roar of its starting fractured the heavy silence. You'd almost forgotten what a motor sounded like. For weeks you'd heard only the voices of Quartzmann and the soldiers, the sound of shovels and picks, the muffled shuffling of the slaves' slippered feet on the ground. Quartzmann picked up his duffel bag and pulled a bottle from it. Clear liquid swilled inside and despite the motor rumbling nearby you could hear its gentle tinkle, its easy whispering voice against the sides of the glass.

Quartzmann handed over the bottle. You tore away the cork and belted some down without even smelling. It was hard, minty tasting, strange to you, but there was no mistaking that bite. You gulped. Quartzmann grabbed the bottle away and the cork from your fingers.

"More when we go, my friend."

He moved to the door, then paused as he corked the bottle. He looked for a last time at the condemned men, then at you. His expression was hard, you hadn't seen that side of him, but you'd sensed it. You had real fear along with the burning down your oesophagus and in your gut.

Then Quartzmann was gone and the job was clear: kill these guys and get a ticket out of here with liquid refreshments provided. The dynamite wired to explode at your feet hardly even figured into the equation.

So here we are again with you and a gun alone in a building in the cold weather with victims ready for the end. But no one around to hold the target steady this time, not that you needed it. These poor guys were whipped, dead for a long time. You were just the *coup de grâce*, really. But I don't know, I guess we all have to ask ourselves what we'd have done, what we'd have gone through. We do. I do.

Did you? I submit you did not. Because I know that you put the gun to the first one's temple and pulled the trigger. Maybe your eyes were closed. But you had to see that the bullet passed through behind his eyes, making quite a mess, and almost hit the next guy in line, who looked like he'd been hit anyway for all the blood and brain matter on him.

They were crying now; there was a noise, whimpering, pitiful. The sound of the shot echoed in the room and didn't seem to want to go away. You stepped over the first body and laid the barrel up against the next guy's head, just above the jaw, pointed outward so you wouldn't hit the last one. This time the bullet drew the man's head and shoulders forward, hurling the body headlong.

Almost home now. One to go. This one sits alone, quaking, but steady. A good target.

Before you positioned the gun, he made eye contact. This startled you. In weeks of working around these fellows, you'd never heard them speak above a whisper, never seen them look at anyone directly. This guy looked at you with glassed-over eyes, his features prominent and widely spaced. By looking at him, you'd never be able to guess his age. He looked old, but he was only twenty-two. It is important that you know his name. Alexandre Kroshnovitz.

Alexandre keeps looking at you, and the fear in your face gives him strength. He sees you don't belong. You sense that he sees every fraudulent thing about you. Knowledge seems to well up in his eyes, pump up his body — he's growing with every second you stare at him. Maybe he can smell the booze on your breath. You panic, push his face around and try to lay the barrel on his temple. He turns back, facing you, boring into your skull with those glassy, dead eyes that see so much.

You push the gun to his cheekbone and pull the trigger. A click. You pull again, no explosion. Alexandre Kroshnovitz has not even winced, he looks at you with loathing — hot, life-sustaining hatred. Even worse, he understands. You know it and it kills you to think of it. This guy knows you. You can see that all kinds of possibilities flash in his head. He balls his fists, flexing. What has he got to lose? You know he's a second away from a fight, and you, you're a drinker, not a fighter. You whip the pistol across his forehead, slamming him backward, then stick it in your belt and grab Alexandre's wretched throat and squeeze.

It is like crushing a garden hose. Things crumble and break, the tissue compressing. Alexandre's face goes red, then purple. He hits at you, to no effect. He struggles for seconds — hours to you — and seems to be drawing on a force outside himself. Maybe you can't beat it. You're having all kinds of doubts. For a terror-filled second you don't know if you're going to be able to kill this guy. Then he falls limp.

You stagger out of the hut. The others are waiting for you in the truck, smiling.

"I give you two for three," said Quartzmann. "You line them up, you aim. Easy." Laughter.

Quartzmann slaps you on the back, gives you the bottle.

"You like this work."

"Sure."

"You drink well. A necessary trait..."

Gulping, you understand what he is talking about.

You walk along as they slowly drive the half-track toward the road, then stop at the edge of the trees. The sapper has fed wires out the back from a large spool. He works quickly, fixing his hot-box. You don't care; the burn is now well-seated down in your guts. Almost to your legs. Soon it will be in your toes. Oh, Heaven. Standing in Hell, you drink in Heaven.

The sapper motions for everyone to duck. "All that powder, blow the whiskers off us, even from here." He depressed the plunger.

Nothing. It seemed a day for false explosions. The man swears, fiddling with his connections. Quartzmann chuckles, points at you and says: "Don't worry. My friend here makes sure nobody gets away."

You might have figured it by now, but this is the important part of the story. It took maybe four minutes for the sapper to redo his work.

Alexandre Kroshnovitz, blinking, recovering, rolls onto his hands and knees, spitting, trying to breathe properly. He looks around. For the first time in four years he is alone. He senses he has to get out, makes for the door but hears the distant rumbling of the truck. He slips through a back window, falls flat on the ground, crawls and staggers away. The sapper finishes rewiring, slips the plunger, and the guard hut is matches, toothpicks and chunks of flesh flying through the air. Some of the wood makes it to the truck.

The concussion knocks Alexandre down at the tree line and he doesn't get up for an hour. By that time you and your crew are far away. Alexandre Kroshnovitz wanders in the woods for a few days, is liberated by Americans and gains back his health. He goes to America, becomes a distinguished scholar, teaches law for many years and writes a book called *Phantom From Solinjberg*.

It's a hell of a good read.

I hate the
Fuckhead.

"...See there was a lot of turmoil at the time. There always was. The country was one vast, thick jungle. People disappeared in it and never came out. They were born to fight and that's what they had to do. And later on the city states fought amongst themselves. And when they weren't doing that they were overrun by almost everybody. French. Poles. Russians...You had to be tough to survive. You couldn't falter.

"It took two thousand years, but in the end it was like surgery; it was so well-defined. Something was gone that couldn't be there and something was there in its place. It's history, Dad. That's all there is to it. I don't know if you've ever thought of it before. I mean, you walk around with it. So do I. It's there, like an extra organ and you should learn to live with it."

15

The drive was through desert country with a heat that chapped Robin's lips. Wherever he touched the car seat it was damp. They camped one night and drove the other, spelling off. Robin was relieved to find Norma an excellent driver, conscientious and willing. Heading southwest on I-40, they stopped for gas and food at a truck stop about fifty miles short of their destination. It was early afternoon in a blazing sun.

He paid for the burgers.

"That's just about the last of the cash."

"My dad can help. He runs a machine shop."

"What? You mean work for him?"

"Yes. He's always got old motors lying around that need rebuilding. Cars to fix. You can do that."

"Yeah, I can do that. How long we planning to stay?"

"I don't know." She bit into her burger. "You can leave anytime if you get bored."

"I don't want to get into this again."

"Get into what?"

"Let's drop it. I don't want another scene. I couldn't take another championship bout without heavy training. You didn't say your dad ran a machine shop."

"Well, he does." She ate, silent.

"Great. Looking forward to getting my hands dirty."

They were five miles past Ascension City when Norma told him to pull a right at the next crossing and go down a narrow paved road that led to a well-graded gravel road. Up ahead in the dry country, Robin could see a collection of buildings. A flat-roofed adobe house, wide and low. Several smaller tin buildings. A large hangar-like structure with open ends.

"This is it," Norma said.

"Looks like a third-world airport," Robin said. He could see little in the rear-view mirror for the ten metre-high dust tail that followed them. "Not a place you sneak up on."

"Daddy likes it that way."

The yard was neat and paved. Machines, buildings, piles of materials, all were sorted in a type of order. No clutter.

Robin pulled up to the house.

Norma was half out of the car when the house poured forth two young girls across a wide veranda. They hugged Norma before she was standing straight. A middle-aged woman appeared and stood on the porch watching. She did not smile, Robin noticed, but surveyed the goings-on with an air of strained tolerance, like something that has to be gotten out of the way before the essential things are done.

Norma turned to Robin, a girl in each arm. "My sisters, Ruby and Dawn." She bent down to the oldest one who looked about ten. "Where's Sue?"

"In the barn."

"My other sister."

"Oh," he said, getting out of the car.

The woman stepped slowly down the front stairs and accepted a hug from Norma.

"Hello, Momma."

"Good you're back. Who's he?"

"He's a man, Momma. His name is Robin. Robin, come and meet Momma."

"A man."

"Yes."

Robin stepped up to the porch. He looked at Norma's mother. "Pleased to meet you."

The woman looked briefly at Robin, at the VW, then turned back to Norma.

"What's Daddy gonna say about a man?"

"I don't know. I don't care."

"You'll be gone sooner than last time, you keep that kind of head."

"You got it, Momma. Where is Daddy anyhow?"

"He'll be by."

The younger sisters had run off to the barn. Norma took Robin's hand and led him in that direction. Her mother stood on the porch, gazing down in a strange kind of resignation.

"This is pretty weird," Robin said, trying to sound casual.

"I told you."

"Yeah, that there were things better left unsaid etcetera. But your mother, she's a statue."

"Wait 'til she gets to know you. Hope you're not shy about rude personal questions."

"Depends on how rude and how personal."

The barn was more of an equipment storage building. By the looks of it, there had never been any animals. There were small rooms, like offices in back. One of these held a cot. Upon this sat a girl of about fourteen. Sue, Robin surmised. She seemed distressed, but happy to see her sister.

"I'm so glad you came back," she said, teary-eyed.

Norma sat down and comforted her. It took Robin about ten seconds to twig to the idea that this was something he shouldn't be witnessing.

"I'll go look around," he said. The girls took no notice of him.

Outside, a pick-up truck pulled in beside the VW and a man stepped out, moving toward the house. Ruby and Dawn, returning from the barn, ran around him, hovered a bit and then went into the house. The man glanced heavily in Robin's direction before walking across the veranda and through the door.

Robin walked slowly toward the house. The two little girls re-emerged and raced to him.

"Daddy says you can stay for supper," said Ruby.

"That's good to know," said Robin.

The family ate at an immense round table. The girls fooled and fussed, excited at Norma's homecoming, and earned repeated warnings from their mother to settle down. Up close, Norma's father, Dan appeared not particularly weathered—this wasn't farming country, people with sense stayed out of the wilting sun—but whittled and toughened by hard work. Norma smiled a lot and did a good job of keeping conversation. Sue did not attend the meal.

Dan looked closely at Robin several times. Robin had a sense he was about to say something. It took until all the fried chicken on his plate was gone before it came.

"Teacher, huh?" Dan said. "All right. I'm fairly liberal about these kinds of things."

That was it. Nothing more during the meal except to ask his wife how Susan was. A hush lowered as the woman answered, "Fine. Comin' round."

Robin volunteered to help with the dishes. The women, Norma and her mother, began the process, excluding him as if they had not heard. Dan disappeared without a word to anyone.

As she was drawing the water into the big kitchen basin, steam rising, Norma's mother turned to Robin. "My husband would like to speak with you in the workshop."

"Okay."

"It's the biggest building," said Norma. "Just go along and I'll be there in a while."

"Thanks."

Robin headed out.

Walking, Robin reflected that it had been good to eat home-cooked food for a change and get off the road, but wondered what was bothering him about this place. Nobody seemed to waste words on anything, least of all each other. There was the sense that the family was a function of its own schedules, the members resigned to some kind of inevitability that precluded any variation, no matter what their thoughts or emotions.

"What can you do with your hands?" was what Dan wanted to talk to Robin about.

"Mechanics. Most every kind, but I haven't done much diesel."

"You know what these are?"

Dan pointed to a cluster of grimy motors at one end of the shop. Many were attached to large gears.

"Some kind of industrial power, I think. Pumps?"

"Sump and compressors. Most of 'em. I got some electrics for conveyors, too. Got a contract with a mining outfit to rebuild 'em."

"Nice job."

"If you want, you can stay and give me a hand."

"Okay, maybe…"

"Whaddya doin' with our Norma? She's a drifter, no damn good."

"I wouldn't say that."

"You wouldn't, huh?" The man moved away, toward the large open end of the shop leading to hard desert, rock and cactus. Robin watched him go, expecting him to return. But that was it.

Back at the house, Norma was wiping her hands on a tea towel as Robin returned.

"Let's go for a drive," she said.

"Okay."

They took off in the dust as the sun was turning the sky amber. By the time they turned off the highway at *Peter's*, a roadside watering hole that Norma insisted Robin would love for its atmosphere, the sky was purple.

"Atmosphere? You sure I won't get beat on by some liberal-bashing red-neck? I can only fight so many good ol' boys before I start losing my looks."

"Don't worry. They know me."

It took thirty seconds for Robin to find out how well. An enormous, red-faced kid of about twenty came up behind Norma at the bar and hoisted her in a bear hug.

Norma squealed and kissed his massive face. "Jake! How are you?"

"I'm great. How're you? You stickin' around this time or you headin' off again or what?"

"For a while at least. This is my friend Robin."

"Pleased as hell, mister. Where you from?"

"Canada."

"Hey, that's great. Let's get drunk everybody!"

Jake had two friends with him. Soon there were pitchers of beer clustered three thick on the bar. A cowboy band played. Robin drifted in and out of conversations with all of them. He sipped ardently on his club soda, trying not to look strange.

Norma drank heartily and laughed with her friends, but was careful to stay close to Robin. The evening went by and the others became more and more blurred to themselves by alcohol and thus more and more revealed to anyone who wasn't drinking, Gradually, Robin sensed that Norma was using him as a shield. Against what he wasn't sure. He had an idea it related to the 'problem' he had been so carefully excluded from knowing about.

"C'mon, baby," said Jake, "let's dance."

"Okay. Just once."

They danced, then Norma returned immediately, sitting even closer beside Robin.

Jake stumbled back to the table. "C'mon, let's go again. Like we used to."

"No, Jake. Thanks anyway."

"Whattsa matter?"

"Nothing."

Leaving it at that, Jake leaned close to Robin's ear and yelled over the band: "Congratulations, buddy. You done what nobody else ever done."

What that meant exactly was not apparent in Jake's smiling face or in his conspiratorial nudge and wink when Norma excused herself to go to the ladies' room.

"Done what?"

"Held onto 'er like that," Jake said.

"Thanks," Robin said.

They drove back in the black, starlit night. No moon. It was so dark the light from the headlights seemed, even on high beam, sucked to extinction in the rough desert and reached only a few feet in front of the car.

"By the way," he said, "where do we bed down?"

"There's a place for you in the barn. Where Sue was."

"Where for you?"

"We'll see."

The cot was made up and ready, the small room made neat and hospitable. This surprised Robin. He had been getting used to the casual non-hospitality of this odd bunch.

He ran his hand down her arm, pulled her close and kissed her. "Let's sit down a minute."

Arm in arm, they perched on the cot.

"I'm not sure about this set-up. Your Dad doesn't seem like the kind of guy who works well with anybody else. I'm not sure I fit around here. I'm not sure I want to stay."

"You'd help me if you would."

"Really?"

"I know it sounds funny after all we went through."

"It sure does."

"Every time I come home it's different. I'm glad you're along."

"Okay. You don't want to tell me a little more…"

"It won't be long. I thought it might be good to get back. It's not. I haven't been away long enough."

"Don't sweat it. It's called leaving home. Lots of people do it. As a kid you think you'll never want to leave Mommy and Daddy. But then like magic when you're a certain age you just turn, and all of a sudden it's like poison, the air around them. You have to go. You only come back for short stabs. You like your own fresh air. It's nothing personal. It's natural."

She looked at him, bemused. "Even when you can't hear me, I love you," she said.

Through the question and slow understanding of what she meant, he forgot everything and kissed her. They moved down together on the bed and it was a hot turn for both of them, clothes off and making love in a fury. For Robin the flow of it was frightening. Amid the uneasy mystery of the woman and the place he loosed a blaze, ramming her wild for a time, catching himself, wanting to make love and losing himself, fucking, then caring again, forgetting.

He faded fast into sleep, but climbed back to the light when Norma broke away, rising out of bed. She turned out the light.

"What...?"

"I have to go, lover. Sleep well."

"Hold it...Why?"

"I have to. Don't worry."

"I'm not worried, don't go."

Robin sat up in the dark. He could just make out her flitting movements, collecting clothes.

"Don't go," he said again.

"I don't want to. But it's for a good reason. I have to."

"It's for a bad reason."

"Silly." She kissed him, pushed him back down and turned.

He listened to her steps fade, and the soft closing of the big door at the front of the building. He lay propped on an elbow for a time, listening to the river-roar of blood in his head.

16

Robin rose at dawn and took advantage of having a fully-equipped machine shop to take a look at the car. He did a lube job. Then he pulled the air cleaner off, took apart what he could and cleaned anything that looked dirty. When he'd put everything back together little Ruby came down to get him for breakfast. Walking to the house, Robin noted that Dan's truck was gone.

He sat by Norma, who looked the worse for wear. Robin put it down to the beer. Dan did not appear. Sue attended, and seemed lighter. Robin stopped trying to figure things out. After the meal he returned to the shed and began a tune-up on the Bug. Dan did not appear all day and nobody seemed to care.

Norma came down and lolled in the shed, handing Robin tools, snoozing in his room.

Robin decided to take a stroll around the property, nosing into the out-buildings, and climbing to the only high ground to see the expanse around them.

In the afternoon, Robin went to Norma, sat on the cot and said: "I think I've got it. What's going on here. I hope not."

"I wish you didn't."

"Nevertheless, it was inevitable."

"I suppose. I couldn't tell you…"

"But you did. By bringing me here. Showing me what your mother thinks of you. What you told me Bobby said. The way you are. The way your sisters are. I had a look at that building back there. It gives me the creeps."

"Did Daddy say anything?"

"I haven't spoken to him. I don't know what I'd say."

"There's nothing you can do anyway."

"Let's just get away from here."

Norma stared into the wall behind him. "Not yet. Sue needs me."

"How?"

She turned away from him, to the wall.

After supper, still without Dan, Robin went to put the finishing touches on his overall maintenance work-up on the car. Ruby came out with a cup of hot chocolate.

"From Norma. She likes you."

"Isn't she coming down?"

"I don't know."

"Oh. Thank you, anyway."

"You're welcome."

Robin sipped the drink, watched the little girl watch him with her clear blue eyes. She would be a gorgeous one, with blonde hair and a fawn-like innocence. He shuddered, trying not to think about her future, wondering what to do, and attempted to sound normal as he said: "It's good."

"Daddy's glad Norma's home."

"He is, huh."

"Yes."

She left, pitter-patters on the concrete floor as she faded into the dark.

Robin finished work on the car, slammed the engine hatch and wondered where Norma was. It was dark outside, he guessed about nine o'clock. Motor noise developed in the distance. Lights raised the shadows at the front of the workshop as Dan's truck entered the yard and pulled up close. For a moment the lights shone directly at Robin. Then the motor stopped, the headlights flicked off and Dan got out.

"How'd you do?" said Dan, walking to the VW.

"Question is, what are we going to do?" Robin was cleaning his hands with a rag, not looking at the man.

"Howssat?"

Robin threw the rag on a bench and faced him.

"You've been dicking your daughters. First Norma, for who knows how long. Then obviously Sue. By the looks of things you leave them until early teenage, decent of you. The younger ones seem undamaged so far. Sue's taking it tough. Norma's a real trooper, seems to take it for everybody else. I don't know what you've got going with your wife, but it's obvious she knows. I'm leaving here tonight and intend to speak to the police."

"You got a problem, fella."

"Hey, I'm not the one who's violating my own daughters."

Robin expected trouble in the irritated silence that followed, but did not expect to see the man break into a sob, collapse against the VW and whine like a scolded dog.

The sight was frightening in a strange way, the sound eerie.

Robin stepped around him and made for the outside. He jogged up to the house, which was dark, and went straight to the kitchen. Norma's mother sat at the table, alone in the semi-dark, lit only by the light from the oven.

"Where's Norma?"

"Gone."

"Gone where?"

"None of your business."

He turned and headed out. Movement, heavy and startling, sounded behind him.

"Why don't you go?" It was a hard, angry shout.

He stopped and turned to her. "Bet on it." He noticed a facial tic, an ugly twinge of the cheek, and the frenzied fingering of a dirty glass on the table.

"Get some help, lady."

"You don't know. You don't know nothin'."

"I know enough."

Robin turned, expecting the glass to come his way, and strode from the house.

He didn't know what bothered him more, the nastiness, the purple-in-the-face sickness of this place, or the fact that Norma had apparently left and gone somewhere without him. He looked back at the house, no lights on anywhere.

"NORMA!" He shouted as loud as he could in the general direction of the house. Then again at the yard, the buildings, the blackness of open land beyond.

Nothing.

In the workshop, the car sat alone in the light. Robin opened a door and went to the back room. Though there was darkness, he could hear heavy breathing on the cot, and a soft whimper. He gathered up his stuff and threw it in a plastic bag. Norma's packsack was there.

He hung back in the semi-darkness, thinking. Dan turned over on the cot. Robin could sense eyes on him.

"The smell of their hair. You know. The smell of their hair; I've loved it so long. So long…"

The smell. Robin gripped the packsack and heaved it into the back of the car. The touch of it was strange. Everything was strange now.

The car started, he slammed it into reverse and geared out of the workshop. As he swung back, up the yard past the house, Norma's mother flashed past his sight, standing erect by the front door.

As he accelerated past her, toward the gravel road, he did not notice the shotgun gripped in strong, wiry hands.

An explosion shattered the rear window of the car and the passenger seat blew forward, spewing fibres in a thick mist along the windshield. Robin spasmed, shocked and stung in the back of the neck. He lost control, swerving hard into a wooden lamppost by the road. The impact mangled the bumper and the trunk lid buckled up into his line of vision. The seatbelt held him back, preventing the loss of his nose against the steering wheel, but as the engine stalled and he recoiled from the jolt, his nostrils were filled with a cottony substance. He had to blow outward to clear his nose enough to breathe. Puzzled at first, he realized it was car-seat stuffing.

Robin paused a moment, resolved to exit the car calmly, trying to take this odd happening in stride. He had the presence of mind to kill the headlights. Upon foot-contact with the ground his knees buckled. His grip on the

door kept him from going down full-force. In the murki-
ness, a distance off, he heard Dan cry: "No, Mother...
Don't..."

Footsteps, running, approached. "It doesn't matter,"
Robin heard Dan say. "Nobody'll listen."

Robin heard another sound. The click of the gun.

"No? You think it's gonna be all right forever?" The
anger in the woman's voice woke Robin from his woozi-
ness. He straightened, his hand still on the car door.

Dan and his wife stood ten metres off, silhouettes
against the bulb-lit yard. The man took the gun from his
wife's hands.

"You gonna do it?" She snarled, a rasping, dry-cat
skirl that made Robin's scalp twitch.

"No. I'm not gonna do it."

"You're not a man."

"Come on..."

"Whining swine!"

"Stop it!" Dan led his wife toward the house, arm in
hand.

Robin shivered, shook his head, clearing, trying to be
sure he was seeing things right. The couple kept walking
away.

Robin groped the back of his neck where the pain
was. His hand came back wet. A scratchy sensation bothered his back. He shook his shirt, rotated his shoulders and
saw there were serious lacerations at his belt line. Glass. He
tore off his shirt and whipped it across his back, undid his
belt and fluffed the crystals out of his underwear waistband.

He bundled up the shirt and pressed it against the back
of his neck, got in the car and tried to see by the dome light
and the rear view mirror whether the injury was serious.

There was one cut that was not bleeding anymore. Listening for sounds around him, from the house or the buildings, he rifled through his bags for a clean shirt. He got out and changed clothes in the driveway. Nobody came. He looked at the car.

The front end looked so bad Robin was sure the Bug would never roll again. He half-heartedly re-started the engine, put it in reverse and was dumbfounded when he was able to back away from the lamppost, wheeling as if nothing had happened. So far so good. Not even any funny sounds.

He cut the motor and got out to survey the damage. The back window was completely gone, laying in a sparkling shroud across the rear seat of the car. The front bumper was bent back and almost broken at the middle. Robin inspected as best he could under the front end. He went for a flashlight and slid under the car. No leakage. He quickly went for the toolbox.

With a crowbar, he managed to wrench the mangled trunk lid back to near its original shape and pull the whole mess apart from itself enough to almost catch the latch. He bound the mess to the bumper with his belt. It would have to do.

He threw the tools back, got in, started up and pulled the headlight switch. One worked. Good enough. He left the yard, kicking gravel as he hit the roadway. He drove fast, jamming the pedal down, and almost lost control on the loose surface.

Where was she?

Lights up ahead, a neon sign, a roadhouse. The clear possibility entered his head. He pulled off the road and drew up to the door of *Peter's*.

Weaving through the semi-crowded tables and across the dance-floor toward the bar, his impulse was to order a drink. He stopped at the bar. The bartender looked at him. Robin did not make a sign, fighting, trying to fend off this ambush on his brain. The music, pounding electric bass and a howling cowboy, forced its way into his skull. The pain in the back of his neck was close now, like a new toothache. He looked away from the bottles at the back of the bar, searching among the tables and standing people. Then he watched the dancers, and there she was.

Norma was dancing with Jake. Robin's magnetic pull toward her and the one coming from the bar were almost equal. But then she saw him, turned quickly away, looked again and stared with fearing and sadness at him. He went to her.

"Let's get out of here." He had to shout above the band and realized that he was angry.

"Forget it."

"Come on."

He offered his hand. Jake snorted, smiling, and looked from Robin to Norma.

"Forget it," she said. "Go."

He could not mistake that syllable. Even through the C&W roar it rang plain.

Go.

He looked at Jake, leering now, his hand low on Norma's back.

Robin fought the rising violence like burning oil in his guts. Then he about-faced, turning his back on them, and went to the bar.

"How much for a bottle," Robin yelled, pointing.

"Twenty-two fifty," the bartender said.

Robin dug in his pockets. He had twenty-five dollars in folding money and a little change. That, plus the dollar or so in the ashtray of the car. Destitute. But he had a bottle. The bartender put it in a paper bag.

Holding the bottle close to his chest, Robin marched across the dance-floor, through the tables and out of the roadhouse. He did not look at the dancers.

Outside, past the car, he went to a far corner of the building and hid in the darkness beyond. With his back to the wall, the violent C&W thrumming his spine and making his chest feel hollow, Robin threw the paper bag away and wrenched off the twist-cap.

The glass was on his lip, the tingle from the fumes in his nose.

He did not hear the light footsteps.

"Hey…!"

The bottle popped out of his raised hand and spun like a trailing, spewing pinwheel in the air before dashing itself to death on the merciless asphalt. Robin turned, swiping at the figure beside him. Norma ducked in time.

"What do you want?"

"Let's get out of here…"

He looked at her, then at the smashed, fuming glass. "I asked you once. You didn't want to go."

"It makes me cringe to see you like this."

"Isn't that nice. Now gimme twenty-two bucks to replace my bottle and get the hell out of my face."

"No."

"Gimme."

"Let's get out of here."

"What happened to forget it and go, Robin. Fuck off and die. What happened to that?"

"Never mind. Let's go home."

Norma took his hand. Robin did not wish to give a hand. He fought an impulse to hit her. Hard. He drew his hand away. She came closer. He grabbed her and forced his lips to her face, grinding. She did not accept him, but stood still while he mouthed her cheek.

"Robin, don't."

"Why not?"

"I know you can do it better. You and I can do it better. Let's just get out of here."

"What about Jake?"

"Fuck Jake."

"I know. What about him, though. Won't he come after us?"

"He doesn't care. None of them do. They know me. That's why I've got to be with you. You don't know me."

"Confusing. But what the hell's going on?"

"I tried to push you away. I guess I was just trying to make it easy for you."

"Nothing's ever easy for me. Ever. Nothing. Get that through your head."

"What's the matter with you?"

"That's a stupid question. You think I'd be here if I knew?"

"I guess that explains a lot of things. I guess you're a bit crazy. Is that right?"

"That's all. I know the problems. I'm fucked in the head about them. I don't know how anybody ever got so fucked over as you. But you're still reasonably together. That's one of the things that's so crazy…"

"Don't talk anymore. Let's go."

"You mentioned that before."

"Let's just do it."

He let her draw him from the gloomy shadows, into the neon-lit parking lot to the car.

"My god, what happened?"

"I told your old man I knew what was going on. Your mother came after me with a cannon."

"Oh my god."

"I guess I wore out my welcome."

"We've got to go back there."

"You kidding?"

"No. We have to. Sneak back. Just for a minute. I need my packsack."

"It's okay, we've got it."

"What?"

"Here."

He went to the shattered rear window and pointed. She laughed.

"Yeah, funny. Real funny. I damn near caught a load of lead in my collar, for crying out loud."

"No, no, just get in. Get in."

"Okay…"

She slumped into the damaged seat, still laughing. He hesitated, hand on the door.

"I still want a drink."

"Get in."

"I still want a drink."

"Robin."

"Seriously."

She stopped laughing. They stared at each other. He looked down, away from her, fingering the door handle.

"We don't have any money," she said.

He kept on fooling with the door handle, thoughtful.

He looked at the roadhouse. A couple lurched out, giggling, the swinging door releasing a fresh rumble of country sound. He sighed, trying not to grimace, and swung down into the car, slamming the door and turning the ignition in the same motion.

A minute later they were in the perfect darkness that desert on a moonless night gives. The dashboard lights gave them the pallor-look of the dead. Norma rummaged through her packsack, rustling papers. She reached above, fiddling with the dome light. Then it was on and he lost sight of the road in the bright reflection. Close to his face, Norma held a hand full of dull green money, big bills, crisp and powerful-looking.

"What the hell!"

"I lied," she said, gleeful.

Robin reached up and turned off the light so he could see the road.

"He keeps it all in his room. Doesn't believe in banks."

"I think you'll convert him."

"I always wanted to rip off the son-of-a-bitch…"

They drove.

"I hate the fuckhead," she said.

17

You and the boys ripped across the Ukraine as best you could; the booming of guns pushed you panicking further and further northwest over road that had been pounded by moving armies and aerial bombardment. Eventually you had to slog the half-track truck across open fields and through thick bush, once in a while taking a chance in the open.

You weren't used to travelling with army people. It was a shock at first when Quartzmann commandeered cottages and the odd scrap of food from the peasants.

One day a Russian fighter swung down over an open stretch of ground. The half-track made a good target and the guy loosed off a rocket, right on the mark. It blew you and Quartzmann out the back and sliced the two in the front into wet ribbons. The truck burned enthusiastically, the bodies sizzled loud enough for you to hear while you were running away, surprised how unmoved you were by the whole thing. Maybe you were turning into a soldier. You weren't that drunk at the time, either. The flyer didn't come back and you started walking.

Since the camp, Quartzmann had taken an even more important place in your life. He seemed to hold an almost perverse interest in you, your welfare, your opinions. He asked you often how you liked your work. When you didn't answer he got mad. He needed somebody who wasn't a soldier to reflect from. You didn't analyse it much at the time, but learned to always give him some kind of positive feedback about what he was doing. One day he killed a farmer who had held out on some food — horsemeat sausage hidden in the floor. Quartzmann stabbed the man through the chest with a pitchfork. The farmer's wife and kids watched the whole thing. Afterward he made the wife make tea. He asked you what you thought.

You said: "Good sausage." You were solid pals from then on.

Quartzmann's orders were to report back to his unit. Where his unit was he hadn't the foggiest. The plan became to outrun the encroaching pincer movement of Russian and Allied armies sweeping up the Eastern theatre. Still on foot, you made it somewhere north of where the *Wehrmacht* was surrounded. It seemed less chaotic. There was a checkpoint; you were both asked to show I.D. Quartzmann talked them out of seizing you for more forced labour by showing them his orders and where you fitted in, telling an officer that he'd take responsibility for getting you back to his unit.

Quartzmann's unit was non-existent by then, consumed by the Russians a week after they'd left you at Solinjberg with your respective assignments. Together, you walked further and reached a village with a headquarters unit. Quartzmann learned his status: unattached. You were taken to a stockade and crammed into a cellar with about a hundred others.

There was little food. Some of the men who'd been there for weeks were dying, looking a lot like your former workforce back at the camp. There was much activity in the village — you could see it from the small windows in the cellar — movement of troops, guns, horses. Despite what many of us would consider a harrowing odyssey thus far, this was the worst it had been. The cellar was a stinking death-hole, with a world going by above your heads and days passing without so much as a howdy-do from the jailers. Hunger was a vicious personal torturer. Sores developed in your mouth and on your feet. You started thinking you might not make it.

After a week Quartzmann showed up, hollering at the guards and banging on the cellar door. He sauntered in with a new uniform on, new badges. He walked among the prisoners, looking carefully at each, tapping the more physically fit on the shoulder. He tapped you.

"All chosen, follow me."

You trooped out. The low winter sun pinched your eyes after the darkness of the cellar. Quartzmann had his small force, uniformed like himself, form the chosen into ragged ranks. He stood tall and puffed up, in front of the troop, hands behind his back.

"You are being offered a golden chance to become soldiers. Only those most proud need choose. Those who are not, back to the cellar."

No one moved.

"*Gut*. You will now be fed."

It was true. Quartzmann had come back and hired

you as a soldier. The idea was fantastic. You had trouble getting your head around it. You'd been a lot of things, but fighter, follower of orders, swearer of allegiances to flags, these were not some of them. But the aroma of cabbage soup quickly wiped away any doubts.

Next came a cold truck ride through the winter countryside. Your clothes were getting thin, but Quartzmann, taking you aside, slipped you a cotton liner for your coat. He also found some thicker boots for you. On the last leg of the trip, he let you ride with him in the cab of the truck.

"Not bad, my friend, eh?" He nudged you in the ribs like an old buddy. "You'll like this kind of work. I know."

Did you think about the peasant with the tines through his heart?

Whatever you thought, whatever you may think now, it all would have been behind you. No one would ever have confronted you with it again, as I'm doing right now, if it weren't for that first day in camp when they gave you a uniform and took your picture. They lined you up, cut your hair and took your clothes away. You surrendered your faded, stolen papers for a little brown book with your face pasted inside. That's what did it, what connects you to all this drama.

You hated the uniform, felt unreal wearing it, like a true alien, a machine. The material clung to you like another skin. You tore it off at the end of each day. Every morning you hunched in your bunk, wishing the day would not start. They were training you to operate artillery guns. The noise was driving you strange. You thought you'd never hear silence again for the ringing in your ears.

Your sergeant was always around, helping his pal. You hated the sight of him. You knew what power he had and how his anger could bring death. The other men figured the connection between you and Quartzmann right away, as soon as they saw you with that coat liner and new boots in the truck convoy. They didn't like suckholes. You took your meals alone or with Quartzmann. You had no friends.

18

Robin and Norma drove most of the night, got a motel, slept, and woke amid intercourse. Robin plunged, driving away from the earth and orbiting, trying to get as far away as possible.

Later, resting, Norma rolled a little away, aligned herself to face him and said: "I hope it never matters. I hope it never bothers you that Daddy was there too."

As he struggled for something to say, Robin fell darkly to the truth. It didn't matter a damn. Not even a bit. He'd known it for years: he could fuck a woman whose father had fucked her and not care. He could do it with someone who had suffered as much as Norma had suffered from sexual violence and it almost made it better. He went cold with the revelation, but was at least relieved that he now definitely knew where this fine person fit into his life. He wondered how far she would ride with him before she also understood. In the same moment, he knew that she already did.

He said, "Why didn't you just tell me straight out about your dad?"

"I don't like to bother people with it."

"After the gun story, it wouldn't have surprised me."

"I guess not."

"Just made it worse."

"I'm sorry."

"Don't apologise."

"It's all I can do." Norma looked away.

"You could have just out with it. I'm a big boy."

She looked back at him, closely. "Would you have still come with me?"

"Yes."

"Are you sure?"

"Pretty sure."

"It doesn't matter?"

"I told you."

"No, you didn't."

"Why do you need this?" Robin shifted in the bed. He faced her squarely. "Why don't you just be who you are instead of making me answer all these direct questions?"

"Don't answer them then."

"You'd be suspicious." She looked downward, away from his weighty gaze.

"No, I won't, I promise…"

He raised her chin with a gentle finger. There was a panicked moment when the inexplicable impulse to laugh threatened. Then he found himself getting hard. He stifled a grin.

"I can't believe you," she said.

"Believe this."

He placed her hand on his growing erection. She grinned.

"I still can't believe you."

"Why not?"

"These things are a dime a dozen." She squeezed and batted it playfully.

"I just want to make love again."

"Really?"

"I can't say it any other way."

And as they did, he knew he could and should say it another way. Even though he had deep emotions for her, admired her spirit and conscience, enjoyed her body, he knew that he was not making love but simply driving. Driving and driving.

Finished, they lay sore under bluish road-lights that shone from the front of the motel. They could faintly hear occasional traffic. They watched the changing shadows on the ceiling above their bed.

The plan was to find a rear window and other parts for a VW Super Beetle. They walked by themselves among twisted and dead car bodies.

Acres of metal shone in the desert glare. Norma climbed to the top of one of the wide ranks of stacked metal carcasses and surveyed the horizon.

"Come up here. It's unreal."

Robin climbed, muttering. They'd walked around the massive wrecking yard for fifteen minutes without even seeing one Volkswagen. Now they were climbing.

She stood atop a baking 1970 Impala, a classic family sedan, the type that reminded Robin of earlier days when fathers had confidence in the future and drove big, gas-guzzling boats with flaring, arrogant fins. He clambered into the rear of the car; it still had a back seat. As Norma shifted on the roof above him, he had the uneasy feeling that the four-high stack of cars was swaying with their weight.

"Look," Norma said quietly. "It just goes and goes."

Robin liked the way he could hear her, though out of sight, in the vast quiet of the car cemetery. There was a faint hum of breeze through the windows of the sedan. He looked out the back, laying his cheek on the metal as he would have if Dad were driving the car somewhere, to the beach on a sunny day with the wind parting his hair. The view was something, he had to admit. All those motoring miles, all those smiles and firm hands upon the wheel. The sun wasn't too high, the morning still comfortable. He forgot to try to see where the imported section might be and gazed, lost, out over the decades of road machines.

The calm penetrated Robin's body. Norma clambered down from the roof, causing a perceptible sway. She struggled at the window for a second, dangling over the twenty-foot drop before managing to swing in beside him. Robin, watching her, thought he might reach out and make sure she entered without mishap, then stopped himself. She was strong and determined in the way she moved, in every way about her.

He reached and caressed her hair. "You gave me a fright, there."

"When?"

"Climbing in. I thought you might fall."

"What if I did?"

"You'd hurt yourself."

"Your point being…?"

"What a toughie. Isn't it okay that I care?"

"You don't have to."

"Yes I do."

"Don't you like the view? I wouldn't have asked you up here if I thought you wouldn't like the view."

"Stop it, dummy. Of course I like the view. It means a lot."

"What does it mean?"

"It's an echo."

"Oh...?" Her face was pleasant with question.

"Aha, now we get to a thing that separates us. The age difference."

"What age difference?"

"You look out there, you see dead cars. I look, I see a family, parents, a little brother, going to the seashore in the hot weather with the windows down. Rushing air makes it hard to hear the radio..."

He looked away, across the metallic vista.

"It's so quiet around here. Like death. The way the wind whispers, the only lonely sound. The sound of memories. The whole time is dead. We who might try to live here are dead."

Norma slid close to him and laid her head in his lap. The seat was long enough for her to stretch out.

He buried his fingers in her hair, caught a faint whiff of conditioner, her smell when she was combing her hair, brushing her teeth. He leaned low in the seat, finding her mouth with his and running his hand inside her thigh. In a moment, her jeans and panties off, she was the way he needed, lying fully back on the ancient car seat, head against the door, back arched, offering. He used his tongue to penetrate her wet interior until he could go no further. He reached, tongue-plunging still deeper, lapping her to crisis, her hands on his head.

The smell, the taste, the joy of it. This did not feel like driving. The endless tunnel, lack of air, closeness to death. A wild act of life. When she came, the spasms forced her head against the door, shoulders against the seat. She twitched and heaved. He withdrew gasping.

He sensed the motion of their automobile-bed. Sharp sine waves from the centre of Norma, penetrating clear to the ground and beyond. Beyond and forever, he felt, or at least as far as this continent went, this land connected by grains of sand and grits of dirt. As far as men wanted women and women wanted love. Love penetrated the ground and vibrated the shadows, reverberating back up through the car bodies and piercing him through his knees. It reinvigorated Norma's shuddering after-spasms, giving him jolts of tightness, then an immediate violent need to enter her. He unzipped and inserted in one motion, suspending himself with his arms over the backseat bed. In seconds the slam-rock motion caused an alarming oscillation in their teetering steel cradle. Vaguely aware of the quirky danger, he was glad his coming took only a short series of motions. He blasted, hollering, into her. They collapsed against each other, sweat-moist, and felt the wavering of their car column steady down and subside.

They found the European section and finished the job before the afternoon heat turned the junkyard tarmac into a giant frying pan. Out on the road again, heading east, Robin struggled with what to do about Dan. He looked over at Norma, watching the countryside go by, enjoying herself.

"When we get to New Mexico, we'd better call about your father."

She did not turn to him, though he could sense unease in the way her breathing changed, and the stiff way she spoke.

"You mean call the cops."

"Yeah, I guess that's what I mean."

A pause. Robin became more nervous with each silent second.

"I guess we should think about this."

"You know I can't talk to any police."

"Why? Because of that California thing? Would they even know about it?"

"I don't know. Maybe."

"Okay, so you'd let your little sisters get abused because of some slim chance you'd be identified on this other thing."

"He'll stop now. You stopped him."

"Oh yeah? I scared him a little, maybe. How long do you think that'll last?"

"Long enough for my sisters to get out of there."

"Hmm…"

Robin drove on, expectant, hoping, to resume discussion. He began to form a vague idea of a long-distance, anonymous call. He remembered the reverberation of gunshot in the car and the zing of shotgun pellets. Out loud he said, "And then there's your mother."

"You said it," she said, on the verge of tears.

Norma did not speak again for many hours.

Driving through the Petrified Forest, trying to make the New Mexico border before dusk, Robin was glad for the experience of visiting a place he'd seen in the movies and only heard about from others. It took his mind away and he hoped it would do the same for Norma. A roadside diner flashed by, old fashioned high-top gas pumps standing idly in front like pedestrians waiting for a bus.

"If we stopped there, we'd probably get involved in some kind of escaped convict, hostage drama. We're just that kind of tragic couple, don't you think?"

"Huh?"

Her blankness was genuine, he knew it without looking at her.

"Haven't you ever seen *The Petrified Forest*? It was Bogart's first big role. Made him into a star."

"Humphrey Bogart?"

"No, Humphrey the humpback whale. Of course Humphrey Bogart. Who else?"

"He was an actor, huh? I wondered who he was... I thought he was a politician. I always get them mixed up, actors and politicians."

"You can be excused. Anyway, just so you know I'm not getting Alzheimer's, Bogart made a movie in the 1930s that was set near here. He played an escaped convict, just about the time that John Dillinger, a real-life convict, was on the loose. He did a good job. Freaked a lot of people out. Anyway, it all happened in a studio somewhere else that was supposed to have been here. Just so you know."

"What's Alzheimer's?"

"Good god, we're at a disadvantage here. It's a disease associated with aging wherein people lose certain faculties — memory and reason being two — as they get older. I mention it because of the vast age difference between you and me. Not that I think I'm particularly old. I mean, relatively speaking, I'm still quite young. But compared to you, in amount of information alone, I'm vastly more advanced."

"Vastly weird, you mean."

"Call it what you will…"

In a small town east of Phoenix, Robin heard a curious note among the other tones of the VW's motorised aria and wondered if there weren't more troubles on the horizon. After lunch at a lonely roadstop, the issue was settled by a shrieking emission on restart, as if the car were being tortured by demons. It was a Sunday with no hope of a real garage mechanic in sight.

A waitress directed them to a neighbourhood workshop a few miles away. They limped the car onto a rutted road and toward a cluster of buildings. Behind a small house, among numerous car cadavers that Robin approvingly noted were mostly Volkswagens, was a toolshed.

A man worked half-visible under a jacked-up Westphalia. Robin stopped the car nearby. Norma squirmed.

"I don't like this."

"Why? Been here before?"

"No, but I know shit when I see it."

"That's what this car is if it doesn't see a doctor real soon."

"Okay," she opened her door and stepped out.

Robin got out and approached the man. Norma wandered off to a pen containing a solitary horse.

"Vhat chew vhant?"

For a moment Robin did not comprehend. The accent was intense, the voice came from a pair of legs under the van and was contorted with effort.

"Car trouble."

"I can hear."

"I think it's the fuel pump."

"Sink vhat you like. It is your flywheel bearing…"

"Okay, it's my flywheel. Can you help us?"

The man slid out from under the vehicle, wrench in hand, and began to clean the tool with a rag.

"It vill cost."

"Of course."

"How much can you spend?"

"Enough. How much you figure it'll run us?"

"The part may not be quite right. I fabricate my own."

"Whatever."

"I vill be paid in cash. No receipt."

"All the same to me."

"Two hundred."

"Really?"

"You are welcome to try elsewhere."

"I guess you got us."

"By the sound, she vill blow up within a mile."

"I wouldn't doubt it."

"Up to you."

Robin shrugged.

The mechanic gestured toward the shop with his wrench. "Vheel it in."

Norma remained well away, feeding the horse, walking far off toward the end of the large pen.

Robin sat around and observed the work. To his surprise, after the initial surliness the mechanic was garrulous and almost jovial. A case of beer was produced. The man's face clouded seriously when Robin refused an offer to drink. He opened one for himself and grimly set about his task.

They talked. Robin found a stool to perch on and eventually asked:

"So what the heck's a guy like you doing out here by yourself on the wide open dry land like this? Far from home, aren't you?"

"This is my home for seventeen years. The old country is not my home."

"Okay. I know kind of how you might feel. I guess there's no future there unless you're already kind of set up, eh?"

The mechanic looked up from where he worked inside the engine compartment and gripped his beer.

"My family held land. We were well off. I left anyway. I could not stand the guilt, all the silly bullshit about the war and all that."

"Oh yeah."

Robin looked around, wondering if it might not be wiser to steer the conversation elsewhere. His eyes sensed something familiar in the darkened rear of the shop. He hoped it was not what he thought it was.

"The world had no idea," proclaimed the mechanic.

Robin saw that a stylised swastika was indeed what he saw, burned firmly into the plywood back wall with a cutting torch.

"Uh, yeah… No idea about what?"

"How the war destroyed a good thing."

Robin struggled for a reply, then let it go. The mechanic went back to work. Silence hung in the workshop while Robin browsed and the mechanic struggled to remove the still-hot engine parts. He worked with speedy skill, not bothering to completely remove the pieces and parts in the way. Robin got up from his perch and strolled to the back of the shop. The burnished insignia became less identifiable as he approached. He saw that an effort had been made to wash the carbon stain from the wall, causing a blurred effect.

He looked again at the man working away and fought a lurch of alcohol-longing. Many weeks since the last drink, he hated that it still affected him this way. The beer case was nearby, open on the workbench.

Before thinking further about anything, Robin stated in a prominent tone, "Yeah, but…there's this small matter of a couple of zillion people who got killed…"

"We were all working." The mechanic spoke as if expecting the remark. He looked up from his task. "Do you know what that means?"

"Well, yeah…sure. I mean, I know you guys were pretty hard up there for a while."

"Do you know what it's like to have no food?" He strode to the workbench and grabbed two bottles from the case. "Do you know what it's like having no pride?"

"Uh…well…"

The mechanic poked Robin's chest with a bottle. "Just be glad you don't. Have a beer." He offered the bottle.

"Thanks but I really can't."

"Suit yourself."

The mechanic twisted off his bottle cap and drank.

"But, jeez," Robin said. "Right wing politics. Reactionary fanaticism…"

"What do you want to do? Change the world or get your car fixed?"

"That's difficult. If you think about it there's no easy answer."

"I will give you a clue. Your seals are completely shot."

"I didn't notice anything."

"No you did not and for good reason. The car was made strong. The car was made so you do not have to do anything with it right away. It was made to drive through deserts and forest and ice cap and keep on going no matter vot. To run on whatever and go to wherever. Even if the driver is a fool. Even if he has something else on his mind. Even if he is drunk or ignorant or even dead…"

"I find the steering a bit funny at times."

"I check it for you."

"Thanks."

"Don't mention it."

The mechanic worked away with a wrench, grunting, mumbling and making car-working noises. Robin went to the yard to see where Norma was. He watched her feeding the horse, and wondered if he shouldn't have joined her. Then he heard the mechanic grunting and thought that in order to expedite the job, he would remain to offer any assistance necessary.

The mechanic was under the car. Robin re-perched on his stool. "You work a lot on the weekends like this?"

"What I can."

Robin surveyed the tools on the bench. "Nice stuff you got here." He had to raise his voice above the clamour of the mechanic's wrenching and grunting efforts.

"What?"

"I said nice set-up you got here. Just like a real dealership-type shop."

"No compressor."

"What? For air?"

"Pneumatic wrench."

"Oh."

"Very expensive."

"I guess."

"Some day."

"Sure. Just keep working. You can't be doing too badly."

"Not bad."

"You got a regular day job?"

"Ya."

"Doing what?"

"What do you think?"

"Okay, so you got a regular day mechanic's job and freelance on the weekends like this."

"It is not bad."

"No income tax."

"What do you mean?"

"Well, you don't report this weekend stuff do you?"

"Report?" He emerged from under the car, regarded Robin gravely and swigged his beer. "What is this report?"

"I mean you don't claim the money you make off jobs like this one. No one would expect you to."

Wordlessly, the mechanic wheeled a jack from the back of the shop and proceeded to crank Robin's Bug into the air. He then gulped deeply from his beer, almost finishing the bottle. He regarded the vehicle closely, running a hand along a damaged part of the front end.

"Despite its wounds, this is in reasonable shape. How long you have it?" He positioned himself on a coastered platform and again slid under the car.

"Oh, hell, a while. I have other cars. Had a van before that. And I had another Beetle too, a long time ago. High school."

"I was twenty-five years old before I had a car."

"Hmm…"

"Goodt car, eh?"

"Good car?" Robin walked casually around the car. "I

don't know if you could exactly use a term like 'good'. These things were a phenomenon, beyond good..."

"What?"

Robin slapped a fender affectionately. "These babies were all we used to drive. I mean, none of us was rich. But almost every other cat I knew could afford a used Bug. In those days a tank of gas for one of these things was, hell...buck seventy-five maybe. And repairs, heck, we did 'em ourselves. Everybody knew something about how to do one thing or another on 'em. My van, I just used to keep oil and gas in the thing and it went and went and went. Bunch of us drove it clear across the continent one time. Just kept going. Picked up and dropped off people along the way. Drove when we wanted. Stopped anywhere. Didn't even have a map most of the time. God, what a time. Sometimes you'd wake up in the morning and there'd be people sleeping around that you couldn't remember seeing before. 'Course, we were all pretty heavy into smoke at the time. We made it to the Coast and hung out all summer, then headed back for school. What a time. Thing had a pretty wild paint job in those days. Had to repaint to sell it. Big peace sign on the front..."

The mechanic rose from under the car, finished his beer, threw the bottle back in the case and opened another. "Almost done," he said. "This is going to cost you."

"Yeah you said that."

"Three hundred."

"Thought we agreed on two?"

"That was before."

"Well, what all's the matter with it?"

"Seals."

"You said that."

"Expensive job."

"What else is there?"

"Adjustments."

"Adjustments."

"Ya. Sorry to give you the bad news."

The mechanic returned to work under the car, beer bottle and additional tools close by.

Robin paced. "This sure isn't like the old days. No time and no way to fix it."

"Do not worry. Your 'Peace Machine' will be running again in no time."

Robin turned his head sharply to look at the half-visible mechanic. He was glad the heat of anger on his face was a private show of his own. He went to the workbench.

"Take you up on one of these."

Robin took a beer and twisted the cap.

"What?"

"Never mind."

While the mechanic continued his work, Robin stared at the opened bottle, raised it to his mouth, faltered, set it down, picked it up again and stood with it cocked against his hip. He looked away, over the tools on the bench and around the shop. He put the bottle down and leaned as casually as he could against the bench.

After an hour, the mechanic slid from under the car, sat up and drank the last of his beer.

"Almost finished."

Robin stood, stretched and moved to where the mechanic had been working. The mechanic released the jack. The car lowered dramatically. Robin, standing close, fought the impulse to jump clear. The mechanic eyed

Robin's alarm, smirked slightly, and pulled the jack away.
He wiped his hands on a rag.

"You got cash on you?"

"Uh huh."

"No cheque?"

"Nope."

"Good. Just a few more adjustments."

He began tinkering at the motor with a screwdriver.
Robin watched, shook his head, smiled and said: "God, that
van, the more I think of it, wow, it got us through some
adventures. It wasn't all good times, don't worry. I mean,
those were strange days. We didn't mean any harm, but
people thought we did. Kindly old grandfathers, guys
who'd bounced us on their knees and given us baseball caps
and bought us hot dogs. All of a sudden we were longhair
freaks with homicidal drug-crazy bug-out eyes who frightened dogs and children. My Grandad threw me out of his
house when he saw my hair. Hated the van, too. Don't know
if it was the paint job or the make, though. He was a patri-
otic Ford man. Hated imports. Bad for the economy, he
used to say. And that trip we took. People treated us badly.
One morning we woke up and some farmer had smeared
cow shit across the windshield. Most of the time we weren't
even allowed to stop and get water…"

"Fascinating. I am sure you had it tough."

The mechanic finished his tinkering and closed the
engine hatch.

"Don't get me wrong. We didn't care. Or if we did,
nobody ever showed it. But times have changed. Nobody
takes that kind of crap anymore. Hell, you should see the
guys now, the ones I still know about. One of 'em's a cor-
porate lawyer. Does he kick ass. One guy turned out to be

a cop. My ex-girlfriend has gone out and made herself a million bucks in real estate…"

"Too bad for you, eh?"

"Well maybe. I don't know; it never would have worked. But the point is none of us take a beating anymore that we don't absolutely have to. We've got memories. Good ones. There'll never be another time like that. But it's over. We all learned our lesson, we don't get kicked around anymore."

"You got three hundred and fifty dollars?"

"What for?"

The mechanic gestured to the car with his rag. "Three-fifty."

"Long way from two hundred."

"Tough job. I do good work. Ask anybody."

Robin dug in a pocket and began counting bills. "Yeah you come highly recommended. My girlfriend lives not too far from here, maybe we should put some of her friends onto you. One guy in particular. He's got a Rabbit."

The mechanic stood with is hand out. "Ya, maybe. Pretty busy these days."

"You'd like this guy. He's as much a fanatic about these cars as I am."

"Then I know I don't want to work on it."

"Great guy. Works for the IRS."

"What?"

"Got a nice little Rabbit, almost new."

"No."

"Three-fifty, eh?"

"Ah…"

Robin handed over a wad of bills. "There you go."

The mechanic stood holding the money. "No."

"What do you mean?"

"*Nein*. Here." He handed the money back.

"Well, hey, you do good work."

"Two hundred dollars."

"What?"

"You win. Two hundred dollars."

"Sure?"

The man nodded, turned away and wiped his hands on the rag. Robin peeled a couple of bills from the wad in his hand and dropped them on the workbench. The mechanic picked up the bottle of beer Robin had discarded on the workbench. He looked at Robin quizzically, then shrugged, gesturing with the bottle.

"Good car."

"I know."

"Good for then. Good for now."

"Right."

Not knowing exactly what he was talking about, Robin did not know what to do with the silence between them. He wondered if the car was ready to drive away.

The mechanic took a sip of his latest beer and brightened. "You know, what was good about when I was young and we had nothing, people were all so friendly. Laughing und singing. We had a sense of humour about it. Nobody protested. We wouldn't have dared. Protest against ourselves? Stupid. No one had time. We were all so busy. Working all the time. My father, how proud he was, he worked and worked. His hands would bleed at the end of the day. Barely time to say hello to all of us. We vorked and shared."

"Sounds okay as long as nobody went hungry."

"Okay? Funny word. Okay. Maybe."

"It sounds like what we were going for, way back then. Didn't work, though."

"Ha, ha."

"What's funny?"

"The way you say it. 'Didn't work.' Ha, ha."

"That's funny? You got one weird sense of humour there, pal."

The mechanic laughed uproariously. "Ha, ha. You don't see it? You, who are strong." He mimed a comic chest-thumping. "The man who does not get kicked around any-more. You work for something…Oop. 'Didn't work.' You give up. Just like that. Hah!"

"Oh, I get it…"

"Where I am from, a man works, he tries to do some-thing, he does not give up."

"Yeah? And the results are plain to see."

"What do you mean?"

"Look at the mess you guys made."

"Mess? Maybe. Maybe not. But the spirit has never died."

"That's bad news."

"Bad. Good. All in the perception."

"I perceive it as bad."

"You don't like your car?"

"Huh?"

"Your car is the living proof of our spirit. You drive it every day. You advertise our ingenuity, our pride, our work and sweat.

"Lot of other things, too."

"Look around you. Seldom does good ever come without some bad."

"Hmmm. You've got a point. A lot of people see dif-ferent things. Maybe Grandad's right."

"Ah, but stick with your beliefs! Don't get kicked

around! Drive it, and to hell with what people think."

"I don't know. That's how trouble like that gets started."

"Whatever. It's your car. It's what you can afford."

"You got that right."

"By the way, you need a new wheel bearing."

"What!"

"The rear driver's side. I would guess that sand got in there somehow."

"I just repacked it."

"Maybe you are not such a good mechanic as philosopher, eh?"

"Shit. Is it bad?"

"It will go for some time yet."

"You sure?"

The man put a hand on Robin's shoulder. His boozey breath made Robin shudder. "Trust your faithful mechanic."

Driving out of the place, Robin did not see at first where Norma might be, but closer to the horse run he spotted a solitary figure far up a low-rising field toward the highway. He had to traverse rough terrain, a ditch and a ploughed field to get to her.

"Is it okay now?" She swung into her seat.

"That's a big question," said Robin, steering for the Interstate.

The driving, sex, and repartee continued across several states.

As did the semi-deserted towns; billboards in the middle of nowhere; immense, empty vistas of the desert; rusting, abandoned car bodies haunting the side of the road. New Mexico was a blur of vast blue-meets-brown landscapes, with friendly waitresses at pie-and-coffee way stations peopled with truck drivers and easy-sipping highway lawmen who, though ever-smiling, kept their sunglasses on indoors.

The Texas Panhandle went by. Then they were almost out of Oklahoma and into Arkansas before the next important piece of conversation occurred. "Where are we going?" Norma asked one day, studying the road atlas.

"Richmond, Virginia."

"Oh…"

Pause.

"I guess I should tell you why."

"Don't I deserve to know by now?"

"Sure you do."

"Okay then."

"I'm sorry. I know it's weird, but I don't know how I can explain to you how hard it is. It's awkward. It's terrible. I don't know if anybody should know something like this. I don't know if I'll even be able to handle it in the long run…"

"For godsakes, spit it out already."

"Okay, okay. Here it is. I'm going — we're going — to Richmond, Virginia, to see a man who's in a home, or an institution or something, I'm not sure. He's gonna be surrounded by people, security types, because they think he's a war criminal. Among other things, he was identified in a book by a guy who survived a concentration camp. He worked as a millwright for forty years and had just retired when this book called *Phantom From Solinjberg* came out, describing him and how he must have slipped out of Europe after the war. Some people put two and two together and he ended up being investigated, accused. Now they're trying to revoke his citizenship and have him extradited to Israel.

"It's all very dramatic. The reason I want to go to Virginia to try to get to this guy is because I've got some pretty strong suspicions about another one of the characters in the book, also described in great detail, except that I don't think the escape from Europe scenario is right. Not by a long shot. I think this second guy was a naturalised Canadian who didn't have any trouble disappearing once all the shit was over.

"Anyway, I've got to get to the guy in Virginia, who's name is Gerhardt Quertzlund, but who they're pretty sure used to go under the name Quartzmann. I've got to get to this guy and somehow talk to him to either confirm or rule out the suspicion I have. There is the possibility that this second fellow, who did some awful stuff too, is my grandfather.

"My grandfather. Who nobody truly knows where he was during the war and who did some pretty shitty stuff while he was here, too.

"Anyway, I've got to go there and see. It's what I've been doing since you first saw me. I don't know if it's the right thing to do but I can't get it out of my mind. I think it might help things somehow. I don't know in what way. If I knew the confirmed god's-honest truth about the thing, it might give me some rest, you know? I mean I don't even know how I am about it.

"I don't think I hate him. I'm not sure I blame him for a lot of the stuff. God knows I've raged. Drank. Argued. Fucked in anger. All those things I hope one day I can just forget or forgive and feel better and not let it get to me or whatever, I don't know…"

Robin ran out of words and drove on. He did not look at Norma, keeping his concentration on the road, trying not to be concerned at her silence. There was a shortness in his chest; he concentrated on breathing deep.

Norma cleared her throat. "Well," she said, "this sure is different."

It was Robin's turn to be silent.

"Different?" he said at last.

"You know my history with rides. Aside from the fatal one, I've had rides who just wanted somebody to talk to. Some of them just wanted a babysitter for their kids. I've been dragged into boring Sunday dinners by people thinking they were doing a Christian kindness. Businessmen who needed someone to take over driving because they were falling asleep. I've had truck drivers pick me up because they were sure they'd score some uppers — I look like the type. Lots of them have tried to fuck me. I never let anybody come close."

Robin was about to query, to ask for clarification, to find out if she was going to ask to be let out at the next town. He wanted to know these things but found he couldn't speak. Even though he was certain of an end. The thought of losing her right at that moment paralysed him. He was sickened at the way he was using her. He knew at this moment he would do anything to keep her by his side, but also knew he would not try to keep her from leaving when another time came.

They drove, saying nothing, and it took a long time for Robin to relax.

19

I did something once, maybe Dad told you about it. The time I got taken home drunk by the cops. There's more of a story to it than that. Poor Sebastian, nobody paid him much attention in those days. Maybe not now either. Anyway, it was in the days before I put it together and got serious about school and quit drinking for a while. There was a good reason why I did that.

Sebastian was about eight. He'd come in from playing in the snow. I must have looked haggard, sitting at the table nursing a coffee and a hangover. He went to the other end and played with an empty milk bottle. I growled at him to stop the noise. I growled at him whenever I addressed him in those days. He went into the living room and Mom told me to be nice to him and that I'd be baby-sitting for the rest of the day because of something she and Dad were doing. I was pissed off but orders were orders and I was trying to be a good kid once in a while.

So that night I went and pulled him up off the couch where he was sleeping and got his boots and coat on. We went out the front door into the dark. Mother called a goodbye from the kitchen. I took the poor kid's hand and hauled him away before he could answer. I decided to try to make the best of a shitty situation and take him to a hockey game. On the way we stopped at a bootlegger and got a twenty-sixer of whiskey. In the alley behind the arena I pulled a couple of good shots from the bottle.

Sebastian just watched me.

I decided what the hell let's have some fun and offered him the bottle. He took it, using both hands. He raised it carefully to his lips. I didn't want him to drink any. I didn't know what to do. I had thought he'd chicken out but the little kid was game. C'mon, we're gonna be late I said to him, hoping he'd back down. He gulped some down and coughed and convulsed. Then he nearly dropped the bottle and I gave him a cuff on the ear and called him stupid.

He was gagging so much I almost had to carry him to the arena. We entered the place just as the game began. The ticket-takers did not check us because of the rush of last-minute fans coming through, did not notice my bulging coat. All the seats were filled except for the high ones in the corners. I tried to lose the kid by speeding up the stairs ahead of him but he managed to find me right at the top. We took seats two or three rows behind the last row of people. I started drinking the whiskey.

I drank with a discipline well-developed even at that age. It was hard going; I had trouble getting the stuff down. I stopped for a minute and tried to concentrate on the game. Sebastian had found a comic book under one of the seats and was happily browsing through it. I snatched it away from him and flung it toward the ice. The book fluttered, landing far down in the crowd. Sebastian hurried down the steps to recover it. I laughed.

After that he stayed several rows down and to the side from me, hiding amongst the people. Whenever I thought of it I'd glance down to where he sat. I was drinking again, force-gulping the whiskey down.

After a while I got interested in the game, yelling things like, C'mon, ya stupid sum-bitch, the puck, ya dumb-ass, hit 'em ya goddamn asshole, and all that kind of rude stuff. I yelled so loud that everyone could hear. Some of the men in the lower seats turned around to see. I jeered back at them. When they looked away I laughed.

Sometime in the third period I yelled something like, Score you fuckin' slobs! Women looked up and blanched. A guy stood and shouted for me to shut up. I swigged at the bottle, then looked around and spotted Sebastian again in the crowd. He was staring at me. When he saw that I'd seen him he quick-glanced back to his comic book. I guess I didn't like the look in the little kid's eyes so I stumbled down and grabbed him by the collar, pulled him backward off the seat and dragged him a few feet on the cold concrete before letting go to steady myself. He got up and I yanked him toward our seats.

We sat for a while before I got the bright idea to put the empty bottle on the steps a few rows away and ball up a program to play target practice. I wound up and let it go, missing the bottle by a lot and almost hitting someone below. I kicked Sebastian in the back of the neck. He pitched forward and hit his forehead on the seat in front. But he didn't cry, just picked himself up and looked at me. Get it! I told him. He scampered down and got it like a good kid and when he got back I smiled and patted his back twice and slapped him upside the head with the third stroke.

Instead of giving me the ball, he turned around and tossed blindly at the bottle. The little bugger hit it. It fell down and smashed loud. The sound startled the people just below and I just about shit myself with rage, slapping him, twisting his arm until he screamed. I was throwing him down on the floor so I could put the boots to him when the home team scored and the crowd reacted with a loud enough roar to distract me. I looked up. The referee signalled to disallow the goal. I forgot about Sebastian and joined the boos and downcalls. Sebastian slipped my grip and ran away to where I couldn't see him.

I started screaming obscenities. The game started again and I went looking for little brother, staggering and lurching. He did a good job of hiding because I gave up after a while and leaned against the rail, watching the game. I wandered back up the steps to my seat. Then a player stumbled and I yelled, C'mon fuckhead, get up! Ya tired ya clown fucker? Ya cocksuckin' scumbag GET BACK IN THE GAME ya slimelicking faggot ya, and other words to that effect.

A few people got up and left. A guy rose from a few rows down and started toward me. He was followed by another. They grabbed my arms and began to haul me toward the aisle. I panicked, whined and snivelled, pleading that my little brother was there. I looked around for him. I wanted him to save me.

They hefted and manhandled me down a few rows and then I wedged myself between a couple of empty seats. Some ushers came to help. Somebody walloped me a good one in the face. They carried me out of the arena. I saw

Sebastian following at a discrete distance. They dragged me down the steps to the inside concourse. My head hit several times. A policeman was waiting and told the ushers to hold me down until the wagon arrived.

Sebastian had to walk home by himself and I caught supreme shit. I hated the little bastard for years. I plotted to righteously shit-kick him someday when I got the chance. I carried that around for years and after a while it seemed to take tangible form, like a picture on the wall or a piece of furniture. Other times it became like part of the air, heavy and sour and difficult to carry. It wasn't until I left home and came back a few times that I discovered how much I loved him and how sorry I was.

I talk to Sebastian all the time now. It's hard to talk about those times, though. I'm sure he understands.

20

The only good thing was a steady supply of booze. In this respect, Quartzmann never let his little buddy down. In fact, on Sunday afternoon stand-downs from training, he made a point of arranging a place you could both relax and take your drinks in a quiet atmosphere, away from the rabble. You were thankful for these oases, even though they were in the company of a paunchy wolf with searching eyes. Quartzmann had an ego that needed constant stroking or he would act like he might tear your head off and use it to play soccer.

From an historical perspective, professionally speaking, it was a remarkable place and time. The famous last stand of the Axis forces, and there you were. The army you were working for, the division you were in, had been formed two years before from rag-ends of other shattered armies: out-of-work officers and men stranded like Quartzmann without units; ex-concentration camp guards;

anti-Communists; and people like yourself. Drifters, with little choice or inclination, but united in a sincere wish to not starve to death. The outfit was called *Halychyna* in the Ukraine, otherwise it was known as the Galicia Division. You told me about some of this long ago but you never mentioned the name. Maybe you never knew it in the first place, or maybe you forgot. The Galicia Division was an army unto itself. When the end came, being full as it was with opportunists and agile survivors, it made the moves to surrender to the right people. Very important.

The Galicia Division fought one engagement with the Red Army in Austria, April 1945. It was your first and only experience as a fighting man. Quartzmann rode along in the cab as you drove your mobile gun, reassuring you that, yes, this was the kind of work you would enjoy.

I think by now you might have been plotting to kill the man somehow. For reasons that remain unclear, he was intent on showing you as rough a time, as gross an experience of war, as possible. I'm sure you'd have run away if it hadn't been for the booze he kept supplying and the fear of losing his protection. Not to mention his innate violence — you retained in your mind the image of a man dying in front of his family, a pitchfork sticking through him. I guess there is a place in this world for people like Quartzmann, but that place would be best far away from you or me. Our violence is of a different kind. Another nature. In a way, maybe you envied the man his outward, honest malevolence, the way he freely manifested his shit into the air around him and on those he considered worthy targets of violence.

Anyway, for the first time the value of this bootlegger actually dimmed in your mind when you saw what he'd got you in for. Quartzmann was in charge of a unit of mobile

77's and mortars. There were rocket launchers, too, but no rockets to load them with. For days you dug in, the spring mud just beginning to dry, bivouacked in damp woods.

Back in the bush again. It must have seemed to you an endless cycle, years of it, slogging through forest, foraging for life, wondering where your next drink was coming from. Did you ever forget about your other life, or was that all you ever thought about? I can hardly imagine all these events. I've struggled to research it all just right, to get a sense of it. But there you were, with home farther away than ever and this war, nightmare of nightmares, just going and going and never stopping. And these characters you'd seen, you'd worked with, you'd killed, you'd drunk with. Who were they, and how did they fit into the general system of things? Did you ask yourself?

When the first barrage came you asked yourself whether death would be clean and swift, or as it looked — horrible, lingering and painful. You and your comrades crouched in the trenches as the plodding, awesome crash of the shells walked closer to your lines. You knew then the quiet, deadly logic of what they had been trying to teach you those past few months, the thorough and scientifically proven method of killing people by dropping high explosives on them, of laying a pattern from which it was near-impossible to escape.

You listened with hands over your ears and eyes closed tight as the explosions, shattering the ground, progressed closer and closer, marching like a murderous giant, one side to the other, covering the space between you and forever in a complete, total scouring of the land. The first shells fell on distant trenches and you could hear the screaming through your hands. Then the explosions were so close the ground punched you like a boxer, in the back, the ribs. Your neck strained to keep your head mounted properly. The pressure in your skull made your brain feel like it would ooze out your ears and pop your eyes. You couldn't believe human beings could suffer like this.

The explosions were still nearer, a train permanently roaring by. The screaming now was coming from you, the only other thing you could hear aside from the blistering crashes. A shell landed metres from the mouth of your hole. Dirt and debris showered down, razor-rough on your face. The next charge did the same.

Another fell close but didn't get you any dirtier. The next one blew some distance away. The giant had walked over. You opened your eyes. The next blast, still farther away, was accompanied by distant shouts and a scream. A flue of dirt and garbage rose straight in the air. From nowhere, someone's arm bounced on the lip of your hole and tumbled to your feet.

So now you've had it; it's all over. You've slipped, finally broken loose and seen the world for what it is, a total game of getting out alive. Staring down at this poor victim's last clenched fist, you could truly see.

You flew out of the trench, yelling. Quartzmann, crawling out of his hole, saw you and smiled. That's the spirit! He pointed to you, turned to the others. Here's a man with stuff, balls, true fighting instinct. He knew he hadn't been wrong about you.

The barrage had passed, but now, through the ringing of everybody's ears, came another sound. Motors. Heavy metallic clicking. Tanks. The rumble of them, in their hundreds, suffused the ground and rattled your shins.

The men swung onto their guns, clearing, cleaning,

loading the undamaged ones and stepped to shouted directions. Quartzmann called to you. You ignored him, climbing into the cab of your vehicle.

"No, my friend," Quartzmann called, running up, "you are in position. Man the breach."

You didn't even know he was there. You fired up the motor.

"Stop! The Russians are that way."

You pulled out in a hurry, lurching out of the trench, wrenching the carriage off its blocks, demolishing the emplacement. Quartzmann was spun around by tearing camouflage net.

"Stop!"

You still didn't hear, driving for dear life.

The roar and crash of the guns covered the sound of your motor as you flew through the camp, knocking down anything in your path not already destroyed by the barrage. Quartzmann recovered and ran after you, grabbing a piece of netting and yelling for you to stop.

You hit a roadway and accelerated. Quartzmann, almost getting a grip in the rear toe points, yelled for some infantry soldiers by the road to shoot you. You roared by, they not knowing what the madman hanging onto your back was saying. You floored the pedal, not caring about shifting gears, you couldn't get away fast enough. The diesel whined but kept pumping out power; there would be no motor failures today. You flashed down the road, away from the battle noise, your knuckles solid on the big steering wheel. You swerved to avoid a bomb crater in the road. The big unretracted gun, high in the air, de-stabilised the truck, making you fishtail, bumping on the rough shoulder. Quartzmann lost his grip, fell, spun into the shrubbery and disappeared. You kept on, driving like the wind.

The battle that day was short. Despite knocking out many tanks, the Galicia Division artillery was overrun and wiped out almost to a man. Scattered elements of the outfit flew back through Austria with the racing Red Army at their heels. You drove the truck another few kilometres before you lost control on a badly shell-pocked road and sank it in a muddy ditch. You staggered through deserted farmland, planning to shed the uniform as soon as you could find other clothes. Then you ran into a ragged column of infantry, fleeing the day's debacle. They invited you to join them in going south to find the British and surrender.

That sounded like a hell of a good idea. Two weeks later you entered Italy and were interned in a holding camp for Galicia survivors.

Quartzmann never showed up, to your elation and surprise. You never saw him again. But I'm sure in your mind you knew he wasn't the kind of man to let a little thing like total annihilation of his unit hold him back. He lived. Thanks, I'm sure, to you dragging him out of the battle area. He later turned up in Berlin, fighting the Americans in the last days of June. He spent some years in detention, denying his identity, telling conflicting stories. Then he got out and disappeared, surfaced somewhere else as someone else, and people are still arguing over who he is.

You spent two years in Italy. The British there were slow in deciding what to do with you but eventually they let you go to England. Getting back to Canada was difficult while the Nuremberg trials were on. Three more years passed before they lifted the ban on the immigration of

Eastern Europeans to Canada. You sailed, landed in Montreal and stood in the immigration office line-up. You passed through, uttering your few words of DP-English, got stamped, approved, passed, and vanished forever on a Montreal dockyard street. Nobody ever saw the man named on your phoney passport again.

The train ride to the Prairies went by like a dream. You caught yourself dozing, then waking, thinking you were in the war again, on the run.

The farm was still there. The neighbours looked at you like you were a ghost, not speaking. The boy, a man now, came in from the fields.

His eyes were neutral. He looked at you passively.

Ten years of his life.

Static.

21

It took thirteen days to wander as far as Virginia. At Robin's instigation, they stopped often to tour the clusters of Civil War sites, parks and monuments. He found Lynchburg full of such diversions. Their progress slowed almost to a stop.

"Why don't you want to get there?" Norma asked one day as they sat in a parking lot near Appomattox National Historic Park.

"What's the matter, don't like history?"

"History is fine. You're not doing what you said you thought you were supposed to do. What's going on?"

"We never tell each other what's on our minds. Isn't that a rule or something?"

"You're bitchy today," she said, getting out of the car.

It was true. Robin walked woodenly behind her as they approached an old building, a former residence it looked like, that served now as a museum. A melancholy had taken him with a strange and, for the present, unmanageable hesitancy. Being near to confirming what he already knew was the truth rendered him sluggish and weak.

The truth. For what it was worth.

She was absolutely right. He wondered if she also saw the fear and cowardice in his dawdling. The feeling was an odd one, like seeing an old friend walking down the street, hurrying down to meet him, then at the last minute becoming afraid, ashamed and embarrassed that they might turn and see you. Robin had done that, slinked away to a corner, let the truth walk far ahead.

The closer they came to Richmond, temporary home of the cruel Sergeant Quartzmann, the closer came the certainty that Robin's grandfather was a war criminal. There it was.

Robin followed Norma into the building and looked blankly at the artifacts: an old wagon, crude military rifles and handguns, grim photographs. Then they came to a large room full of well-restored artillery pieces. He remembered the detail of the Galicia Division military history he'd read, with its descriptions of ordnance, fire capabilities and the narrative accounts of the three major battles.

At another Civil War park, The Wilderness, one wall of the museum was a huge, ghastly photograph of a stack of uniformed bodies, melting in the southern heat, the aftermath of one of the severest battles. A tour guide droned on about the political instability of the Southern seat of government while walking them through rooms of portrait paintings and photographs. Dazed by the stark imagery of the 'wall of dead' scene, Robin was not listening closely, but woke up when the guide announced that "at this time the South recognised the value of possible reconciliation and a proposal was made to remove the major bone of contention. Specifically, a motion was put forward

in the Richmond Assembly to exterminate the slave popu-
lation and thereby make mute the major difference between
North and South. The proposal was voted down..." The
words stiffened Robin's back. There was a ripple of chuckling, thin in the crowd but present nonetheless, at the
words 'voted down...'

The coldness Robin experienced seemed generated by
a world-sized deep freeze, hanging, he felt, over his head.

Robin and Norma walked onto a wide field, lushly
grassed, and struck wordlessly off to a far ridge of trees,
away from the other tourists. They walked for fifteen minutes in complete silence.

Finally, it was she who spoke. "This is one of those
times when you tell me more weird stuff and fuzz up my
head. And we start driving again like crazy. Right?"

"Nope. You know the whole story."

"There's nothing more? Then why are we going so
slow?"

"Are we going slow?"

"Do you want to get to Richmond or not?"

"I do. But there's no rush. What do you want to do?"

"Whatever. I don't mind going slow. I don't mind
going fast. I just want to know that we're actually going."

"We're going."

"You're sure?"

"Yup."

"Good."

They walked. He looked at her. "The truth is," he
said, "I'd like it if *you'd* say where we were going for a
change. I mean, I don't like giving the directions all the
time. The trouble is in me. It's not yours. You don't have to
be here. I want you to be, but..."

"I like it."

"What? You like my directions?"

"I don't want to say where. Let's just go where you want to go. If I think of a place, I'll tell you what direction to drive."

"That's assuming I have a direction."

"I know how weird you are about it, but I know you want to do this."

"You do, huh."

"Yes, and I think you better hop to it."

"You're pretty tough."

"Yes I am and I know you are too."

"I'm not tough. I'm not even vaguely rugged."

"You're vaguely crazy…"

He managed a laugh.

They were in Richmond that night, checked in at the Confederacy Plaza Motel 6. The traffic rumbled by on the freeway. Norma watched game shows. Robin sat at the little desk and tried to write out his thoughts. It was important to remain focused. Blocked, he considered the traffic rumble outside. Like a growling monster. So close to Quartzmann, he thought, this noise should have been caused by the proximity of an immense monster, not by gas-burning vehicles full of normal, unsuspecting people on their way to and from work.

An immense monster.

The next morning they drove past the institution where he resided. Robin explained to Norma about the status Quartzmann had in this country, about the legal things, the stripping of citizenship, the extradition to Israel. They were holding him in a makeshift secured section of a long-term care facility. It was a vast complex of large buildings, gardens and a park-like setting with wide, well-maintained lawns. They noticed several official-looking cars, men in suits and uniforms.

"Who are those guys?"

"FBI probably. Could be CIA. Maybe even MOSSAD."

"Who?"

That did it, right there. Robin was nailed to the wall with it. He looked at Norma. Here was an intelligent person, clued in about most things that mattered. God knows she had more on the ball emotionally than he ever would. But she didn't know old movie stars, and she didn't know who the Israeli Secret Service was or why they would be guarding an ailing Hyphenated-American old-age pensioner with a thick accent. Something in her face jolted him, returned him to that old determination, the certainty he had had waking up in his rented house back on Vancouver Island a couple hundred years ago. There was ignorance in her face.

Robin confirmed after a few phone calls that getting near Quartzmann was going to be a problem. The old man was feeble, worn out after forty years of steelworking and determined beer swilling. Voices at the end of a few hospital lines told him Mr. Quertzlund was not available for visits.

In the evening, Robin and Norma watched Quartzmann on the news being wheeled from the courthouse. A uniformed deputy swung a heavy door shut on a reinforced van. They watched witnesses leaving the hearing. An elderly widow, dressed in old-country black, was whisked nervously away by her grown children. The pain of testifying to ancient atrocities showed clearly on her face.

"Maybe you should tell them you're family."

"Naw. They'd know his family."

"Distant family. Long lost nephew or something…"

Robin chuckled at the irony of it. Long, long lost nephew.

The next day Robin went to the institution, clutching a bouquet of flowers and a book wrapped in gift-paper. With only vague plans in mind, he wandered the hallways, eyeing the nameplates on rooms, going down lists of residents. Nothing brilliant occurred to him, he found nothing he could use.

He waited for a Saturday when there would be no court. He walked the corridors again and this time found a room that was being guarded but had not had any such attention when he'd been there during the week. He let himself out through a door leading to the grounds. It was a beautiful day. He sat on a bench in the middle of a large garden area. People moved around casually, visiting aged and infirm relatives. White-coated workers passed by, wheeling residents. Robin decided to gamble a wait.

Time.

Maybe only a few hours, maybe all day. Maybe not until tomorrow or next week. Maybe never, but it was the only thing he could come up with, sitting there in the sun.

He waited until almost the end of visiting hours, the early evening, changing places several times, walking around, trying to act like he was either on his way to or from a visit, trying not to attract attention. He telephoned Norma.

"Is it going to be okay?" He could hear the jumble-buzz of the television behind her voice.

"Yeah. I think so."

"How are you?"

"Nervous. But that's fine."

"Can I help?"

"I don't think so. Not today. If I have to come back tomorrow maybe you can come, act like my sister or something. Get dressed in a Sunday outfit."

"I don't know..."

"Just kidding. What's on TV?"

"Sports."

"No game shows?"

"I'm getting pretty bored."

"I know. This isn't your kind of road scene, is it?"

"It's okay for a while."

"I hope it's not too much longer. It can't be."

"When will you come home?"

For a second Robin didn't know what she meant.

"I'll be back at the hotel before dark."

The next day Robin and Norma showed up at the outside visiting area, dressed in an attempt to look like they'd just come from church.

Norma wore a skirt and pantyhose she'd bought as soon as the K-Mart opened. She walked jerkily, slouched, uncomfortable. "I swore I'd never wear this kind of crap again."

"Throughout life you'll find you do things that give you the damnedest pain in the ass, you wait and see."

"Watch your language, it's Sunday."

"In the heart of bible-thumper's country, you're right. We could get kicked out of this place."

"'Specially you. Somebody's going to bump hip to this thing. They'll remember you from yesterday."

"That's what you're here for. It'll confuse them. Buy me some time. It can't be long now..."

They watched people, residents, medical staff and others come and go. They moved to a shaded bench, out of the sun.

A few minutes after noon, a uniformed guard appeared, holding a door open for a wheelchair. Robin's breath caught. Quartzmann appeared, bundled in his chair, pushed by a suited man with sunglasses. They rumbled past, the suited man quickly scanning the crowd, and headed for a far area of unpopulated lawn.

Norma hadn't known what they were watching for, but noticed immediately Robin's stiffness and shallow breath.

"That's him?"

Robin nodded.

"Well, let's go."

"It's not that simple."

"Sure it is." She rose.

"What'll we say?"

"We want to talk to this old man, that's what we'll say."

"It's not that simple."

Norma walked off in the direction of the three figures, now stationary a good distance off. Robin unfroze, seeing her go, and loped along behind until he caught up.

"I haven't thought it through... gimme a minute."

"The time is now, Robin, we can't hang around this bone-yard a whole lot longer. It's depressing. I want to get back on the road. I'm tired of daytime TV..."

"Shit..."

"I'm tired of every goddamn thing, Robin. Let's get this over with. A joke's a joke, okay?"

"Fuck, I don't know..."

Norma paused, pointing. "Now, there's the guy. Listen to me. You want to talk to him. Let's go do it and get it over with."

Robin had no retort. They resumed walking.

Robin wished for an eternity of walking, new strength and willingness in his legs to walk forever, never to get there, but to walk and walk. His life was a horror as he and Norma approached, close enough to see the bored, dazed expression on Quartzmann's face, the wariness of his guardians watching him, their alert, authoritative movements as he and Norma got closer and closer.

The trio became aware they were being approached. The suited one came to meet them, ten yards away from Quartzmann. He did not remove his sunglasses.

"Hold it right there, folks." He flashed a badge. "Federal agent. I'd like to ask you to stay clear of this area while we're here."

"We want to talk to this old man," said Norma stridently, pointing to Quartzmann.

"Impossible," said the agent.

"Why?"

"That's classified. Now…"

"What is the matter, Ferguson?" From the wheelchair Quartzmann's giant head reared, his stiff voice boomed the words. Robin could see the old man was following the scene closely and with amusement. "You fear my assassination? Not this little girl." Quartzmann smiled widely at Norma, his eyes gleaming slyly.

The agent turned slightly, but kept his eyes on Robin and Norma.

"Don't interfere." He looked at Robin. "Who are you?"

"I'm...a journalist."

"No press allowed. There's a court proceeding..."

"We just want to talk to him," interrupted Norma.

"Ferguson," roared Quartzmann, "let the little girl come. What harm is it? What harm?"

"Be quiet." Ferguson wasn't losing his cool, but his voice was firm. "Now it'd be best for everybody if you folks just stepped away from here. You don't want trouble. Believe me."

"What harm, Ferguson?" Quartzmann persisted.

No answer. Robin, Norma, Ferguson and the uniformed policeman, who stood a little to one side of the wheelchair, all stood silent. Quartzmann chuckled.

"Remember our deal, Ferguson."

"The deal doesn't include this." Ferguson's eyes never left Robin and Norma.

"It does, as of now." Quartzmann's voice had taken on weight. His words were now orders. "Do you hear? Anything can be in the deal, Ferguson."

"No way. Who are they? Baader-Meinhoff? Jewish Defence League? Everybody wants you, old man."

"Some to rescue and some to kill. Poetic, is it not, Ferguson?"

"Quit babbling. Do you know them?"

"We're just people," said Norma.

"You hear the girl, Ferguson. They're just people. And I will speak to them. And if I don't, you will not learn the things you seek to learn. Many will travel free. Many will elude your sick little game. I will speak to them, Ferguson."

"Shut up!"

Ferguson had still not lost his cool, but Robin noticed a glinting of sunlight off the sunglasses for a split second, as if Ferguson were twitching his ears. Quartzmann laughed again.

Ferguson stepped closer to Robin and Norma. "Let me see some I.D."

Both dug in their pockets. The uniformed officer gently laid a couple of fingers on his holstered pistol. Ferguson looked at driver's licenses and Social Insurance cards, carefully comparing the pictures with the faces before him.

"What's your business here?"

"History," Robin blurted.

"Let me see the little girl!" Quartzmann roared.

"Please turn around and spread your legs," said Ferguson.

With expert speed, the federal agent frisked both Robin and Norma thoroughly. Robin could see curiosity on the faces of a number of people watching the scene from afar.

"Turn around." Ferguson's voice was as flat as pond water. His sunglasses did not twitch. "Three minutes. Then you're gone and you don't come back. Your names will be vetted. We will trace your whereabouts. If you are not who you say you are you will hear from us."

Ferguson let his statement sink in, looking ominously at Robin and Norma. Then he stood aside and motioned with his head for them to proceed toward the wheelchair. Norma went gamely and arrived a few steps before the hesitant Robin. Quartzmann smiled widely. Close up, Robin could see the cold in his eyes and was repulsed by the way the old man's lips curled, looking at Norma.

"Let me touch you," he said, reaching for the girl.

Robin noted now the stiffness of his accent. Quartzmann reached and gripped Norma's hand. He greedily caressed her arm.

Norma, overloaded, pulled back, revolted. Then Robin woke to his opportunity. Forgetting any pretensions of finesse or dramatic intro, he abruptly produced the identification booklet his grandfather had given him and thrust it in the old man's face. Out of the corner of his eye Robin saw the uniformed officer move a step closer, hand on weapon.

Robin held the book to Quartzmann, open to the picture and the name. He studied the man's expression. For a moment there was no change from the rapture Quartzmann had shown at touching Norma, but slowly, then quickly, a transformation. The eyes grew wide, the nostrils flared. Quartzmann stared at the picture, then at Robin, then back at the picture. He gasped, almost formed a word with his mouth. Robin, lip-reading, tried to translate. But then the massive countenance changed again, to a controlled, impassive mask. Quartzmann looked away from the book, momentarily at Robin, then away.

Robin did not take his eyes away from Quartzmann, though he knew he now had all the information he needed. The fact that he did not want this last piece of information, the last and final and most damning of all the gathered facts and impressions, did not diminish its impact.

But one more question. One that had not occurred to Robin until now, when he'd seen up close the death-red gleam in this criminal's eyes. He fought a shiver of mortal fear and strained to keep his voice steady.

"Did you ever look for him?"

"Ferguson!" Quartzmann growled. "Get them out of here."

Quartzmann reversed his wheelchair and turned away. Robin looked up, saw Norma staring, the uniform watching intently, and Ferguson, some distance away, watching the people now collectively peering over.

With one last look at Quartzmann, gravely watching the ground in front of him, Robin took Norma's arm and marched past Ferguson. "Thanks," he said.

Six minutes later they were in the car, headed to the motel. Robin saw immediately that they were being followed. The unmarked car kept a discreet distance, but Robin never lost sight of it in the rear view mirror.

Norma shifted in her seat, thoughtful. "What do you think that guy meant? 'Many will go free and wander,' and all that stuff?"

"I dunno. Some kind of bullshit arrangement where he gets something in return for ratting on other Nazis, who knows."

"What did you say to him? That last thing, I wasn't listening because the guy with the gun was freaking me."

"I asked him if he'd ever tried to find my grandfather."

"What did he say?."

"He said what he'd have to say if he didn't want them to find any more witnesses."

"Oh."

They approached the motel.

"This is bad stuff," she said.

"Let's get the ever-loving fuck out of here," he said.

22

Their escort was still with them when, after having stopped, hurriedly thrown together their things and checked out, Robin sped out of Richmond and took the first exit heading north-west. He drove, gripping the wheel with bluish knuckles, for most of the afternoon. At the West Virginia line they were still being followed. He stopped at a rest station, went to the men's room, came back out and crouched at the open passenger window. Norma woke from a light road-sleep.

"Mind if we just drive around for a while?"

"What?"

"Just around. In circles. Until we get rid of the government."

"Whatever."

They turned south. Then the next day, east. They found a beach near Hampton Roads and picnicked into the evening. When Robin went to get a bottle of mineral water he saw that the government car that had been across the parking lot was now gone. The next day they drove clear, turning north.

They were now on their way to Robin's home and it seemed strange and bad. Norma read magazines and dozed. Her detachment gave Robin some of the earlier neurosis he'd struggled with when she'd been preparing to leave. The uneasiness made him drive quickly, impatient to be there and see it through. Approaching the border Norma slept most of the time, even in daylight. She had a talent. He envied her. He drove quicker.

The VW motored its way from the Customs booth on the Canadian side of the Manitoba-Minnesota border at Emerson. It was seven-thirty in the evening. Robin drove smartly, knowing where to go for the night. The place was about ninety kilometres away over main highway, ten more over secondary, then six down a lonely prairie spur through fields and summerfallow. He noted that harvest had recently been done, the earth-smell rising from the evening-cooled road allowances, and there were the forlorn levelled fields spanning the darkened horizon. Norma, waking, looked around, discomfort smeared on her face.

"Where are we going?"

"Night's coming. We've got to start fresh in the morning, and there's a place I've got to go. It's important."

"Fine, but why don't we get a room someplace?"

"We can if you want to. But just indulge me a bit, okay?"

"Hmmm…" She rubbed her eyes and looked around. The fields were vast, the flatness of the land like no other they had seen. A few lonely buildings occasionally stood out on the landscape.

"It's just here." Robin slowed to turn and swung onto a rutted farm trail, a blot of dust forming behind them. After a few minutes the trail took a wide turn and traversed a culvert. Around a grove of trees at a slight rise in the land they could see the remains of a wooden barn. Part of the roof was gone; the ancient trusses stuck into the sky like skeletal fingers. Robin slowed the car, approaching, and drove across what once must have been the farmyard, now simply a flat spot where the meagre grasses were not quite enough to prevent a rise of dust from under the tires.

"Here it is," said Robin, stopping the car. He did not turn off the ignition.

"Here is what?"

"Part of the story."

He watched her look around, noticing her knuckles, white on the door handle. She shuddered slightly and pulled a sweater close around her shoulders.

"Why would you want to come here?"

"You should know me better by now."

"I guess. It would be so like you to come and rub your nose in it."

"Don't be bitchy. I just wanted to run over it again in detail, so I don't forget anything."

"Didn't you forget to cut the motor? Why are we sitting here wasting gas?"

"Oh, right."

Robin put the car in gear and inched ahead, toward the gaping former door of the barn, now a wide and jagged black hole.

"We're not going inside that thing!"

"Relax, it's sound. Been here for at least seventy-five years."

"It's too spooky!"

"It's okay. I want to get out of sight, anyway. We'll spend the night."

"This is too weird, Robin."

He laughed, easing the car through the broken doorway, pausing slightly to pull on the headlights. The illumination made the interior seem commonplace. They saw the broken timbers of the stalls, the several stout upright columns still holding the loft and roof skyward. He pulled the car forward onto the uneven dirt floor and cut the motor. The silence of the place was an immediate pall. Robin switched off the lights. They sat listening to the ticking contractions of the car and waited for their eyes to become accustomed to the darkness.

"God, this place is creepy."

"That's what I thought, too, when I first saw it" He leaned to slip his arms around her. "The things I found out, the things I know about it. I had a hard time just looking at the place on the map. But I guess I figured it's the old get-back-up-on-the-horse-that-threw-you phenomenon, or some such like it. Anyway, I came here quite a few times to bear out the research, and then started just coming here to overcome my fears. It's downright Gothic in here right now, isn't it?"

He waited for a response, then realized she was weeping quietly in his arms. Never having seen her issue so much as a tear, even with the sadness she carried, he was taken aback. He kissed her cheek, and behind her ear, holding her as close as he could in the twisted posture of the car seats. She shuddered again and accepted his enfolding arms and the warmth that came to her back as he cuddled her. They remained, clutched together, as the last light of the evening crept away, and the sections of the exposed roof stood as dark ribs against the starry sky.

When he felt her body ease, either with comfort or resignation, he said: "I guess it's a positive part of getting old or something. The unearned ability to occasionally see tough things you weren't able to see when you were young and stupid."

"I hope you're right. It's too hard to keep pretending I know what I'm doing."

"You've had that happen too, eh?"

"Don't be silly. You know about me. You know everything."

"Sure, I know a lot. I never hope to know everything."

"That's what makes me sad."

"Give yourself a break. Give us all a break. Get by on what you have. It's what everybody does."

"What I have isn't good for me."

He had to let that one stand. After a while, loathing to disturb the now comforting silence, but needing to relieve his bladder, he loosened himself from her, and opened his door. The coolish air dissipated the humidity created by their breathing inside the car and filled it with a reminiscence of animal smell, like a worn-out leather jacket. She stirred, donned the sweater that had been hanging at her shoulders and opened her door. Robin stepped to the mouth of the black building, seeing by the moonlight, and unzipped as Norma stepped past him onto the prairie and looked around.

Norma walked a little and unhitched her jeans. Then both just stood in the murky farmyard. Robin, about to zip up, watching Norma yank panties and jeans to her hips, immediately stiffened, and allowed his cock to grow out of its confinement and reach into the static atmosphere of the deserted farmyard. He stepped toward her and enfolded her with his arms and acquired with his lips her presence.

Norma balked slightly, retrieving her face from his.

"I don't think so."

"What's the matter?"

"It doesn't feel the least bit right. I told you I don't like this place."

"Relax. You'll like it fine."

He nuzzled her earlobes. When she protested no further, he moved to kiss her mouth, tenderly, then more insistent.

He gripped with both hands and carried her in the uncertain darkness to the curved rear of the car, placing with care the back of her head against the gleaming new glass of the rear window. They kissed and struggled, he with his inverted hand and fingers inside her panties, she with the unpeeling procedure of lowering the tightish jeans enough for entry. He gripped the panties, pushed them down and inserted past, but encountered dryness.

He pulled away, and sought her clitoris amid the tight folds of cotton, nylon and labia. He touched, teased, ran his finger deep, then out again, spreading what moisture there was around the softening entrance, then working more insistently on her until his hand came away moist enough and her legs splayed wide enough for his second attempt.

He slipped in, ramming up tight until the stress of cloth and muscle prevented closer contact.

Thus they coupled in the gloom, with the un-braked Beetle rocking in the abandoned barn. Robin knew that the circle of his heritage in this place was becoming more complete with each second. Because they had not made love since before Virginia and they had been growing uncertain these last days of their place with each others, the heat of the intercourse now was beyond precedent. They dripped with perspiration, Robin's back beginning to glow with ache as he plunged more urgently into her.

Then it was done, with a squeaking announcement from the stressed wheel bearing of the VW, sighs from Norma and Robin and the surprising howl of some far-off coyote. Or maybe a dog, Robin thought, easing back, carefully disengaging himself from Norma's body and her clothes. He embraced her with a loving kiss, running his hands along her back, discovering with his fingers the air-vent furrow weals along her shoulderblades and lower.

Wordless, they went about the movements of camp. Robin got the flashlight and showed where the tent would fit nicely on an unruined portion of the loft, the section still under a roof. They climbed and disrobed, sliding into the tent, the sleeping bag and to each other with a quickness that belied Robin's confident toss-off of the spookiness of the place.

He had never actually spent a night here on his previous visits. Drifting off, he resisted the ghosts: the sound of gunfire, the whimpering of dog and human, the cruel silence, the smell of distant hay, ruined wood and animal blood. He listened instead to the rhythmic intake and expelling of Norma's breath, her quite murmurs as sleep encroached, the deep respiration on loss of consciousness. Before he slept, the well of his feeling for her reached its deepest, surprising him in its clarity and power, his chest filling with the energy of caring for her. Holding Norma in his arms, he was almost able to forget that on the morrow he intended to wreak a violence the nature and effect of which he was uncertain. Unable to disengage the thought, he struggled to think of something else. His mind whirled and he shifted in his sleeping bag, hoping to sweep away the vertiginous whooping of his consciousness and vision. But the tiny star-pricks visible through the tent material began to form shapes, shining a terror spun cinema on his retinas, squeezing his brain. He closed his eyes, almost in panic, and hoped that darkness and silence would take away his horrors. But the swirling colours and night-shapes of his eyelids only made things worse. He opened his eyes, shifted, cleared his throat and let Norma move slightly away in the sleeping bag. He realized as he grew cold that in reassuring and making things safe for her to relax and sleep in this terrible place, he had robbed himself of the security to do so.

For a few moments, fighting the terrors, he missed the comic irony of the situation, then allowed himself to consider it and forced a mirthful chuckle at his goose-bumps, shortness of breath and irritating tightness of scalp and throat. Then he knew with sadness that this was the only time he could remember actually having given of himself in any sense in any relationship. The revelation made him smile, then grieve. He developed a tear in one eye. It rolled down, was replaced by another, and then the other eye welled and saw little through the curtain of salt. He sobbed quietly, concerned at waking Norma, but consumed now only with grieving. He turned and laid his face to the tent wall, collecting tear water at his little place in the sleeping bag.

Unable to stop, Robin cried for himself for a while, mourning the loss of so many years. Then he wept for the tears of the little boy he knew had suffered such anguish within these walls. He cried for his father and the dog and the dying grandmother and the drunken grandfather. He cried for all the things these people never had and never would have and then he cried again for himself. Weeping profusely face down, he knew he was making a considerable mess of things: the bag, the tent. He imagined his tears soaking down to the time-scoured wooden planking of the loft, soaking still through the fibres, down the walls, into the flooring and to the ground. A seeping leachate of tears, flowing in a steady river down to the soil and spreading out, around the abandoned barn, through the long-forsaken foundations of the earlier buildings.

Morning brought sunlight through cracked timbers. Robin rubbed his eyes, found he had worked his head out of the tent-flap, inspected the rotten slats above them, and wondered what had been in his mind. Some looked so feeble in this light they created a fear in Robin that he might have been foolish to trust their weight to them. There was a screeching of birds and sounds of the wind. Norma stirred and poked her head out with his.

"Oh god. I thought it was a dream but it's really true."

"Yes, dear. I have brought you to nirvana."

"Don't even joke…"

She wriggled and emerged, gathering her long T-shirt nightie around her, shivering, and grabbed for jeans and sweater in the tent. "It's too fucking cold to camp out on the prairie anymore."

Robin shivered also and did not move. Though he said nothing, he heartily agreed with her and was stilled with a touch of depression that the season was over. Many things were over. He tried not to darken too much with the coming day's chore.

Norma scampered down the ladder and went out, toting toothbrush case and water bottle. He sighed and moved around, gathered his clothes and donned them standing in the loft. He looked down to where the car was parked below in the centre of the barn. Something in the quiet of the place, and the resonant memories, lulled him into a reverie. Then, snapping awake and anxious to get on with this day, he collected the tent and sleeping bag, dropped them onto the roof of the car and climbed down. Packing the things in the back, he remembered that he'd have to lift the seat to get what he needed. He cursed his earlier dawdling, hoping like hell he could do it before Norma got back.

Norma finished her morning hygiene in the nearby grove. She walked back to the barn and saw Robin fumbling in the back seat. He slid out with the gun in his hand, a solid piece of blue-black.

"What the hell is that?"

"Nothing. You weren't supposed to see this."

"You know about me and guns."

"This has nothing to do with you."

"What's going on?"

"I need it. Just this once."

"I'm outta here."

"It's not what it looks like."

"You're crazy."

"I just need it for effect. It's important. It's part of the story."

"I'm not interested."

"Oh come on…"

"Save it."

She was busy now, digging through the debris of the back seat, gathering her things. The quickness of her movements, the sureness, dismayed him.

Robin spoke over her packing. "Lookit, ah... I'll tell you about it. I'm seven — you gotta listen to me — and I'm wandering around trying to find something to do. His house was old and stuffy, I didn't like the place..."

"Save it, Robin."

Norma lurched herself into the packsack, swaying, averting her eyes. Robin thought he saw a tear. She looked across the clearing toward the rutted path to the highway.

"Don't come after me this time. Seriously."

"Doesn't it hurt you, turning away like this?"

"If you don't know, then this has been as stupid an exercise as I'm beginning to think it was."

"All those miles."

"There's more where they came from." she said. "Goodbye Robin."

"I don't see how you can do this."

Norma sighed, looking down. "Look, it's not a good idea. You know it. I know it. We knew it would end. You like to get in a good space about it once in a while, but it won't last. I just stayed because I told you I would. I wanted to know where you were going. I wanted to compare it to where I'm going. But never mind now. You've got things to do."

"Sure, but... This is a hell of a time."

"It's the time for me. I can't help it."

Robin had nothing further to say. The gun was like a piece of hot charcoal in his hand. He tossed it into the car and it bounced on the driver's seat.

Norma stepped close, pecked him on the cheek, and

walked off. Her steps were silent to him after a few metres, so he couldn't even listen to her fade away. She was out of sight in another minute, going where she knew she had to go. Away from the bad stuff. Not necessarily toward a solution, but away from the bad stuff.

Robin was confounded to realise he was crying again for the second time in less than a day. He wept, and wondered why, embarrassed by the presence of the birds who went silent and watched him. When Norma had rounded the stand of trees and slowly sank from vision, he found the quiet of the birds and all the elements around him intolerable. A terror cut deep lines in his back, like a claw. He stumbled, shocked at the pain and his lack of defence to it. Recovering, hands out to break a fall, he began to run.

When he saw her again, she was running also, at first awkwardly with pack and gear in hand as fast as she could go, then unlatched from the burden and springing like a gazelle toward the road a thousand metres ahead. He puffed and pounded, desperate, swinging his arms and wagging his head in a comedy of athletic effort, trying to gain ground, fatal of mind and soul if he did not. He gained, not because of his speed as much as the fact that the deep soil at the side where she wavered sucked a running shoe from her foot. Her limping, struggling progress slowed eventually to the point she turned around and waited, hands on hips, lips drawn. As he came near, she dropped forcefully down, ramming hands into the lumpy soil and rose again, firing dusty clots with accuracy at his face.

Robin stopped when the first dirt-clump hit his chin, forcing grit into his open mouth, stinging an eye and making him swerve to a stumbled landing in the dew-moistened ground. He coughed, raised an arm to ward off more volleys. The missiles continued, covering his hair with dirt, filling his face with brown caustic film. He found it fine to just sit there, arms over his eyes, doing his inadequate best to defend himself. Eventually he took calming refuge in a gathering sense of self-pity.

The bombardment ended. Robin heard Norma sobbing as she righted herself afoot, bent over with exertion, hyper-breathing to a fretful composure. He opened his eyes and tried to squint the dirt away, shaking his head, fluffing his grit-loaded hair. When he was standing and could bear to let in the daylight, he saw her, back up the trail a ways, ram-fitting her tossed shoe. Then he rubbed his eyes some more, heard her pass him close by and jog away.

He thought long of something to say, then realized a sense of relief at her distance. When he looked up, Norma was far down the path, making steady progress toward the open road.

23

The elder Wallenco sat covered with blankets in the morning light of his back garden, staring into the middle distance. Robin walked around the house, could hear the housekeeper working in the basement, washing clothes. He sat by the old man. It was just as he knew it would be, though he'd not seen his grandfather for some time.

The old man looked at Robin and smiled.

"Do you know who I am?" Robin asked carefully.

Grandfather turned back to his un-focused gaze.

"Oh you must be Robin." The voice came from the house.

Robin looked up to the housekeeper, leaning from the door.

"Uh, yes…"

"They said you were on the road already, probably coming here. It happened three weeks ago. They just let him out of the hospital yesterday. It's nice of you to come."

"What's wrong with him?"

"You don't know? He's had a stroke, poor thing."

"Oh…" Robin looked back at the old man. Then he pulled a chair up close and began to talk.

When Robin had finished, the afternoon shadows were long. The housekeeper had been out several times, serving tea, then lunch, asking if Robin was staying for dinner. Eventually she left them alone. Robin's throat was dry.

"Look, Dad...

"...I know what you're going to say, I mean, I know you don't think much of my ideas. That's okay. Everybody's entitled to their opinion. I knew I didn't have that much, just all by itself. I mean, he said he spent the whole time hiding out in the village. It could have happened that way. People could have hidden him out. The place was wiped clean in the summer offensive. They didn't take many prisoners at that point. You either fled or you died. So there's no way to prove or disprove his story. But the look in that guy's eyes, when I showed him the picture. It took a lot to get to him. They're trying to extradite him. Lots of security guys around. Probably some FBI. Maybe even MOSSAD. Anyway, it took a lot of doing, but I got to him, showed him the book, the picture. He's old, kind of out of it. I said: Who is it? Is that him? Is it?

"...And he didn't even hesitate, he rolled his eyes over at me and I saw that look. There it was. The last bit of proof I needed. I didn't want to believe it, but there it was, the only one left who could have known Grandad, and there he was looking at me like he was back in the camps, ready to put another bullet in somebody's brain. I'll never forget that look. All you guys have it. You've got it. I've got it, when I want it. Maybe even when I don't, I don't know. I hope not. I don't know...

"Anyway, I stumbled out of there. Short of breath. Light headed. It wasn't a surprise. I mean, I knew. But it was a shock *anyway, like when somebody dies after lingering a long time. It still hits you. So I drove around, thinking. I had to do a lot of thinking. I drove to the Georgia Coast and slept on the beach for days. I don't want you to think, like you always do, that I, like, sprung into it without thinking, opened my big mouth and made a fool of myself. Stuff like that. I didn't. It took a lot. When I made up my mind, I was walking through the museum at The Wilderness, that's a place where they had one of the Civil War's bloodiest and had to stack the bodies up in the sun for weeks after like melting cord wood. When I made up my mind I got in the car and drove straight to Manitoba, almost without stopping. Damn near killed myself. That would have been interesting.*

"The minute I figured it out, the second I made the decision, somebody died. Somebody, him or me, was going to get it... No. That's not right. It happened way before that... Anyway, Grandad was a deadman. That's it. Finis. I drove, steadily but not fast, right up there, right up to his place.

"It was just after noon. A clear day, still warm from summer but getting that tinge to it. Still nice enough to sit out in your backyard with just a house-robe on. There he was. The housekeeper was working in the basement, I could hear her working the clothes dryer. I walked around and faced him. He looked up. He was surprised at first, but then he saw the look in my eyes... He almost smiled. It was familiar to him, after all those years. Even though it was a horror he saw in my face, at least the familiarity of it brought him something. I hated that. I hated everything. It flowed through me. He saw it. Aimed at him.

"I told him to get up. He obeyed. I gave him back his I.D. booklet. He looked at it, then at me. I told him to start walking. He didn't want to. I looked at him again. He started walk-

ing. *We went out to the alley. He only had slippers on. He said he was cold. I said he should be. Serves him right. Serves him right. Walk. WALK! We got to the end and crossed the street to that little park and down into the gully with the little stream running through and the trees. Along a path. Into the woods. It was a week day. School day. No kids around, I said stop. He obeyed. I looked at him. I said I'm giving you a lot more than what others got. A reason. Some explanation. A natural fair order to things. Your life won't be an open-sore question of why. You'll know. You will. You know, don't you? You know. Don't you? DON'T YOU! And you're getting it from someone who knows. Everything.*

"*He looked at me and then at the water going by. He looked down at the book in his hand. The tears started. That surprised me. That surprised me. Maybe he'd seen it work. I guess the walk was too much for him. Too much like some kind of ritual he'd seen before. And the look. I'm sure he'd seen that before. He let go. Went to pieces. Sobbed so hard down into the mud that it sounded like his lungs coughing out. Physical distress. Grotesque. Turned into a lump of death. Right in front of me. As if he'd been dead a long time but didn't know it. Corrupted into mud. A history of mud. Mud. He crawled there and died. I didn't once touch him with my hand. Just looked at him...*"

24

He would have taken the gun from his pocket and held it to the old man's head, but he thought it might be better to close his hand on the loose throat. The sponginess of his grandfather's flesh made him immediately sick. He closed his eyes, wishing for something else, wishing he wasn't himself, Robin, in this place, in this time.

His grandfather gurgled, spittle leaving his lips. He stared at Robin, light beginning to appear where before there had only been glassiness. His lips, straining, tried to form a word.

Robin sensed his grandfather trying to speak, opened his eyes and tried not to be weakened by what he was seeing.

Grandfather, turning purple, mouthed a word, managed to make a sound.

Robin struggled, knowing now it was hopeless. Especially with the old man saying what he believed to be his last word. He didn't have it in him, he knew. Cursed or not, Grandfather would live.

He let go his grip. His fingers left white impressions on the greying skin.

Grandfather rubbed his throat.

25

Robin's only thought was: who do I have to kill to get on this ferry?

There were three cars behind him as they began loading, and a million cars ahead. An attendant far down the line motioned for forward movement. He revved the VW nervously, until a cloud of blue exhaust obscured the car behind.

The ferry took in all the cars in front of Robin except one. After a pause, that car went too, but they still had not closed the doors. Robin rubbed his bruised head and tried to have faith.

It was evening, almost night, and this was the last ferry leaving the mainland. He had to be on it. He was lucid, more than ever. Everything was finally clear in his mind. He'd had twenty-five hundred kilometres of sullen driving to organise things.

The attendant arced an ear to his shoulder-attached

walkie talkie, then nodded to Robin. He drove onto the boat and was relieved that it would be tonight he spoke with his father.

It was autumn and the leaves were turning. Despite the cool air, the VW was overheating badly as Robin pulled up to the house, a shadow of oil-blue smoke following him close and constant. He thought of all the distance the car had covered. Considering its hitherto committal to retirement in the weedy backyard of a rural house, its longevity this two months was astounding. Robin sensed, as he turned off the ignition, that maybe the car had wheezed its last. There would be no restarting. Neither he nor car had the heart. It was going to take his all to get through this night. He reached in the back and drew out his heaviest sweater, put on a jacket too and left the car.

Around the back of the house there was the smell of cigarette smoke on the breeze. The scent of beer. Robin ascended the stairs. In the semi-darkness his father did not look up as Robin stepped to the sundeck and stood by the tattered deck chair.

He knelt.

There were the bristles of the neck above the heavy coat, a rasp he had not known since childhood, and the smell of sweat from working in the yard; but Robin Wallenco's memory is full of the sensation of mixing their tears, across his cheek, in a hot smear that burned beautifully for days.